Dead Comic Standing

Karen Vaughan

Order this book online at www.trafford.com
or email orders@trafford.com

Most Trafford titles are also available at major online book retailers.

Printed in Victoria, BC, Canada.

ISBN: 978-1-4269-2400-2 (sc)

*Our mission is to efficiently provide the world's finest, most comprehensive book publishing
service, enabling every author to experience success. To find out how to publish your
book, your way, and have it available worldwide, visit us online at www.trafford.com*

Trafford rev. 1/6/2010

 www.trafford.com

North America & international
toll-free: 1 888 232 4444 (USA & Canada)
phone: 250 383 6864 ♦ fax: 812 355 4082

Dead Comic Standing

He had it coming
He had it coming
He only had
Himself
To blame.
If you'd have been there
If you'd have seen it
I betcha
You would
Have done
The same!
From Cell block tango –Chicago

ACKNOWLEDGEMENTS

I would like to thank the following people for ongoing support: My family and friends as a whole, but mostly Jim, my fantastic husband of 6 yrs. and 2 more years for just getting used to me. It is Jim who stands behind the counter at work and tells everyone; "My wife is a writer!" The Vaughan /Munro cheering sections have been great. They weigh and measure my head weekly to make sure it's not getting too big. My daughter Heather also encouraged me to keep it up.

My fantastic editors: Irma(Saskatoon) and Jeremy(United Kingdom)—who better to edit a book than a retired teacher and a fellow writer?

I also want to thank Haley Milan for fantastic cover work for this book.

As much as I loved writing **Dead on arrival**, as it was in a sense my first born; Dead comic standing was a labour of love too as it combines my love of writing and stand-up Comedy.

Thanks also to my Pogo.com cheering section, and contributors for great comic material and inspiration. It was this particular contributor who wanted to be a "victim" in the novel and I wrote a routine for him based on his renovation woes at the time as well as a day in the life of a retired sailor…Thanks Squid!

Marcus—the Australian dude who saves Shelley from Gord—is a friend of mine who generously donated $100 cad to our United way fund raiser to have his name mentioned in this book. However I didn't think this was enough exposure based on the amount he donated so his character will be featured in a future novel.

Suzanne entered a draw for $2 and wanted to be a victim so she, Suzanne Goodale is a comic and a victim in the story

Prologue

Present Day 2008

The glass slammed down on the bar.

The barkeep filled the glass and passed it to the dude.

"Good show" the bartender said, nodding to the comic on stage.

"He's okay, but I've seen much better," the stranger replied.

"You know comedy?"

"I **was** comedy, years ago. Then I started my own club, hosted the best up-and-comers. I guided Carey, and Myers, on their way up. I was the **Simon Cowell** of the comedy world. I discovered more new talent than Cowell can shake his finger at."

"So what happened?"

"I lost it, son. I lost my faith in humor. Too many bad things happened to accept that laughter can pull you through the worst. Sometimes it can be a curse."

The stranger looked up at the comic who was finishing his routine, before turning back to the bartender. "That kid probably does have talent. He could be destined for *Last Comic Standing*. The problem is I am just too jaded to see it."

"So what actually made you lose your vision?"

The man took a sip of scotch, and said, "My wife died of cancer—a quick death. We didn't see it coming. You'd think that would be enough for a guy to have to deal with...But **then 5 years ago,** some asshole lost his sense of humor, and all hell broke loose."

CHAPTER 1

Summer 2003
Back in the day

An up-and-coming comic was just exiting The Laff Attak. The comedian usually left through the alley after his sets, usually two per night, 30 minutes per set. Like other wannabes, he worked two clubs per week whilst working part time at an upscale Coffee Emporium. This guy didn't want to spend the rest of his career as a part-time Barista /Comic. Oh no, this dude had plans, he was going to be the Robin Williams for the next generation. Well, skip the 'Na-noo-Na-noo' bullshit that Robin had to tout, in his early years.

In the meantime, bills had to be paid and the comic had a wife to support as well. Debbie worked as an insurance adjuster for a huge HMO management company. She technically supported him and his "hobby". At least it was a marginally paying hobby.

The young man walked around the corner down another alley, a supposed short cut on his way home. He feared nothing, although he would never have let Deb do this, day or night. Her argument was why should he? Did he think he was "Iron man" or something? The young dude lit up another smoke, a filthy habit and Deb hated it. Another reason she thought he might die young. She just didn't get the part about a good smoke, after coming off stage. Comics had to be the worst chronic smokers. He had to do it here because once he stepped into the house, no more ciggies. He might as well smoke now 'cause Deb wouldn't let him smoke after sex. Smoking brought him back from the adrenaline high of being 'on'. No matter what shit hit you throughout your day, you hit the stage running with a smile, ready to show the crowd the time of their miserable lives. He stood in the shadows taking a few pulls on the Camel, dropped it and ground it into the asphalt with the other discarded cigarette butts. Debbie, as much as he loved her, had her phobias. She was convinced that some guy would jump out of the shadows and knife him to death, when, in reality, the worst killers came wrapped in cellophane and cardboard.

The next step he took into the alley was his last. A hand holding a butcher knife came out of nowhere. If this weren't the end for real, he would have found a place in his act for the scenario. He felt the knife blade plunge into his stomach, and he went down on his knees, and then fell onto his back.

"Fuck man, if you want my wallet, just ask." Dave was gasping for air.

"It's not about the money, asshole. I just didn't know how else to tell you......"

"What?" Dave croaked weakly.

The stranger grabbed the hilt of the knife, and yanked it out of his victims gut.

He looked straight at him and said,

"YOU JUST AIN'T FUNNY!"

Then the killer slit the young man's throat.

The room was packed. People were lined up at the bar three deep, and all the tables were full.

Jeffrey Beals, the owner and operator of Comic F/X was

looking forward to a good night. His headliner, Phil Vetters was a real crowd pleaser for sure. He was more concerned about Shelley, the new girl starting tonight. She auditioned well, and Jeff had no doubt that she had talent. However, Shelley clearly admitted that her club experience was limited and most of her experience had been in an auditorium setting, doing comedy for educational purposes. This worried Jeff. Shelley was a small girl, and guys tended to eat people like that up, especially after a few stiff drinks. Great prey for hecklers and perverts.

Jeff tried to keep society's baser elements out of the club. However, some just seemed to slip through the cracks. They walk in seeming quite civilized but once a female comic hit the stage, all vestiges of humanity escaped through their assholes.

Comic F/X was full of yuppies out for a few laughs. The club was a brightly lit establishment. There was no smoking allowed and there was a three drink minimum rule. The basic premise was to serve up good drinks and provide quality entertainment. Jeff wanted people to come back time after time, to see the rising stars of tomorrow. He hoped Shell was one of them. Jeff had heard she came from a tough neighbourhood, a white girl surrounded by Hispanics and African-Americans. It was everyone for themselves and one had to develop a thick skin and a strong backbone.

Shell was doing her initial sound check on stage.

"Hear the one about....."

"Never mind the jokes sweetie, just show us yer titties."

"Hey guy what's your name?"

"Who wants to know?" Shelley shielded her eyes from the spotlight to see the person who had addressed her and spotted a large man sitting at a center table. Oh god no, why couldn't hecklers be gorgeous? Why were they always butt friggin' ugly as well as obnoxious? So if she had to put up with this moron, she might as well have fun with him. Maybe the toad would get the message and back off.

"Well pal, I just don't open my shirt for just anyone. I like to be on a first name basis with my voyeurs, if ya know what I mean?"

"If I tell ya will ya take it off?"

"I don't know, by the looks of you, you seem to have a bigger rack than I do."

"You Little Bitch!"

The guy was steaming as the audience watched her dismantle his ego one line at time.

"Whoa boy, you better put on your big boy pants to use language like that, you wanna take your potty mouth and go to the washroom?"

Jeff was watching the impromptu exchange, and decided that Shelley could handle herself. Gord-o was a dog, but Shelley was having an easy time having him neutered. If Gord-o had gotten out of hand, Jeff would have had him thrown out on his ass.

"Very funny girlie—God gave you a sense of humor —'cause you just can't please the boys. Gord-o can teach you what you need to know."

"Well Gord-o, what you can teach me wont take more than two minutes."

"Au Contraire, sweetie, I could have you yelling Gord-Oh by morning."

Gord-O was giving back what she gave him.

"No doubt, loser, it would take you that long to get it up!"

The audience was enjoying the impromptu exchange between Shelley and Gord. There was a lot of laughing and clapping. Gord-o was starting to look the fool. Something he hated, especially at the hands of a chick.

"You freakin' cow! No one makes me look like an ass, and gets away with it!"

"Gordie, my dear, you don't need my help to look like an ass. You're doing a good enough job on your own."

Jeff didn't need to see any more and signaled the bouncers to expel Gord from the club.

Shelley came off the stage, and headed for the bar. She signaled Dave to send her water with lemon.

Jeff approached her. "Great warm up. You made short work

of him. I have seen lesser men crumble under him onstage and then get the crap beat out of them for being a pussy."

"What did he do, sit on their ass?" she retorted, "Thanks for the props, but if ya knew what a shit he is, why did you let him go at me?"

"Sorry I know it was a shitty thing to do, but I had to be sure you could handle heckling. You passed. I had him removed anyway. I want you fresh and relaxed for your set."

Shelley nodded her thanks, and admitted he was getting to be a bit much.

"I have four brothers with a brain between them, I can handle it."

"So I saw, damn fine job."

Jeff and Shelley took a seat at the side. She went on in thirty minutes. Jeff explained that he did well to have a civilized crowd most of the time. Gord was an exception to that rule some days. Shelley had given back more than Gord could handle, and Jeff feared he wouldn't take kindly to being singled out, and might retaliate. He reminded her that there were always the bouncers, and that he had a zero tolerance for harassment of his talent pool.

"If you're worried about the ape trying to get handy with me, don't. I have a black belt in Tae Kwon Do and a can of mace. I can outrun the gorilla, and my 4x4 SUV is one scary little mother. I wanted to thank you for the break here; I appreciate the chance at the club scene."

"You have great chops kid. You'll be great. Stick around and watch Phil after your set, he's a real hoot."

"Sure but right now I better get onstage, before you fire my sorry ass."

With that she went back stage to wait for Jeff to open the show and properly announce her.

Hey, great to be here. My name is Shelley. A little bit about me. I am the youngest and only girl in my family. My four brothers have a lot in common; they share one brain between them..... Actually only three of them are idiots. Dumb, Dumber, and Dumber still. The fourth was born with a penis and a brain. Naturally my mother was shocked.

The audience tittered at this.

Many people call me a butch. At first I thought it was because they meant to say bitch but just couldn't spell. Then I realized they were calling me a Lesbo.

Why are men threatened by a woman with good looks and a sense of humor? They figure you can't be funny and get a guy. So if we make guys laugh, it means we're gay? One guy I took home just to prove him wrong. We were humming along just fine til I laughed at his weenie. After that, he let his buddies know I was a dud in the bedroom. He said I might be funny, but he was sure I liked girls.

More laughter from the audience; Shelley was killing them.

I love animals; I guess I would have to, being raised with the four primates. Dinner in our house resembled feeding time at the monkey house. I know I know…it's not nice to compare the boys to a bunch of chimps. The chimps have a bigger shot at getting a college degree than those animals. The older three attend clown school and are starting at The Shrine circus when they graduate. The one with the penis and the brain has a Masters in Psychology.

I have never been married, but I lived with a guy for six months. The only reason that the individual in question is still alive is credited to the fact that I look horrible in orange and I didn't want to be the prison bitch, of some chick named Hildegard.

Honestly the names some people give their kids, they're just asking for trouble. Imagine burdening your offspring with the name of Hildegard, she's bound to commit crimes—"Come to mommy, Hildegard ---sure she ambles straight into your arms and thwack— you never saw it coming. Just think of her plea of guilty based on getting a shitty moniker at birth.

Norbert is another name that should be avoided at all costs. You're going to have a child with a shit load of psychiatric issues based on childhood bullying. So right after my mom read a book about what your kids' names mean, she stopped calling Bobby, Bonzo.

Well it's been great. I'll be here until Sunday or whenever Jeff hands me a pink slip, whichever comes first.

The audience ate the act up and were standing and whooping for more as she left the stage...

Shelley bowed and went backstage to grab her purse so she could leave right after Phil's set. She felt good after her fifteen minutes of fame. She was no longer a Comedy club virgin. She had lots of material to use and hoped Jeff would give her a bigger set down the road.

Chapter 2

Two miles away, Constables Mike Borneo and Lissa Cassway were on shift, when the call came in.

DB found in alleyway near Sutton and Frank - Stabbing. Meat wagon's been called. Detectives are at scene. Please assist.

Lissa responded and directed Borneo to the location.

"Just when we thought it was gonna be a quiet one."

"What do you want, Borneo? It's Friday night in Edmonton. We'd wonder what had happened to the perps, if there wasn't any crime."

"I would just like to go home one night and not have to wash the smell of death off me, or try to forget the look of an old lady who had just been mugged on her way to get a pint of milk and dog bones."

"Sorry to disappoint, Mikey, but this is gonna be an ugly one."

They got out at the scene and crossed themselves, a ritual they had adopted at every death scene. "Here goes another one," said Mike

"God rest the poor soul, and damn the perp." This was Lissa's response.

Uniforms and crime scene techs were all over the place. Lissa and Mike reported in and helped out with crowd control. They spoke quickly with the D's on scene while holding off the rubberneckers.

Detective Vince Vetters, and his partner Myra Swift were standing over the victim.

"Ah Borneo, Cassway, thanks for responding; this is a bad one. Vic is a card carrying comic, Dave Feener. He was taken down with a knife. Deep gut wound and a slashed throat. We're waiting for ME Watters. The crime scene unit's looking for evidence and a possible weapon, no luck so far."

Swift cut in, "Vic hasn't been dead long. By the look of things, robbery wasn't a motive. Vic still has his wedding ring, and a wallet full of cash and a credit card, all his ID is accounted for, as well. We did find a Playbill near the body for The Laff Attak."

Borneo cut in, "What do you need Cassway and me to do?"

"Go over to the club," ordered Vetters, "talk to Petra James, she's the manager. Tell her Vince Vetters sent you. Ask if Feener worked tonight, and did he have kin. She knows me and she'll help you out."

"Ok Lieut," nodded Borneo. A thought occurred to him then, "Hey, aren't you Phil Vetters brother?

"Yeah, he's the baby, always was a bit of clown."

"Well, we're on it. Come on Lissa. We might just get some comic relief out of this."

Borneo and Cassway left the scene.

"So," said Swift, "we know the cause, but what's the motive?"

"Some one is missing a sense of humor?"

"Not funny, Myra" retorted Vetters.

"You have no sense of humor Vinnie."

"Yeah I know they gave that to Philly. I got the smarts."

Myra laughed. "Now that's funny.

"Shut up Swifty," was Vince's reply

Lissa and Borneo walked into the Laff Attak. The comic onstage spotted them straightaway.

"Hey Ron," he said, "I know my shit is bad but you didn't have to call in **the Heat**"

The audience turned around and laughed at the cops.

Lissa and Mike shot the comic the thumbs up sign and waved the bouncer over.

A bouncer approached and they told them they wanted Petra. After they flashed their badges at him, he pointed them toward the rear of the club.

Petra James was at her desk, going over the books and upcoming talent bookings.

Lissa knocked on the door. Petra looked up, motioned them through, and offered them seats.

"Sorry for barging in but we have some rather disturbing news," said Borneo gravely, "Detective Vetters asked us to come over and tell you."

Petra nodded. "Have seat officers; did one of my comics kill the audience with bad jokes? Sorry bad humor. I can't do the stuff they do. I just hire them. Vinnie sent you?"

"Yes he did and it's much worse, I'm afraid" said Borneo. "We found a Playbill next to a dead body in the alley less than two blocks from here". Borneo picked up a similar looking program from Petra's desk. It was from that night's line up, and featured Dave Feeners' mug on the front cover.

"That's Dave!" What did he do? "

"That's just it Ma 'am--- It's what was done to him." Reported Lissa

Petra covered her mouth and removed her glasses. "Oh God, damn this is bad. What happened? "

Lissa replied that Feener had been stabbed maliciously, but could give no further details pending a full investigation.

"Shit, shit shit. Damn it to hell, this is so messed up. Pardon me, he was on tonight; killed the audience totally. In comic speak that's good. Fresh talent, and now he's gone." Petra was getting misty-eyed as she spoke.

"Did he have any problems with anyone here tonight?" asked Lissa. "Did anyone heckle him during his act?"

"No one that I saw; he handled them well, had a great rapport with everyone. Why would someone do something to him?"

"The police will do their best in busting whoever did this to Dave. We don't know why he was targeted."

Petra cut in here. "I saw a bit of his act and there were no real offensive parts to it that would tweak any ones anger; he didn't ride the political, sexist, race or religion wagon which is bound to piss someone off.

"Maybe someone just didn't like the act in general, but I see no reason to slash him for that alone."

"We need to question the audience and staff," said Lissa, "see if they noticed anyone a bit off tonight. Even if they didn't heckle Dave, they might have had an issue with his act but didn't want to call attention to themselves.

"We need to know if you knew if Dave has a family so we can notify them ASAP."

"I can get that for you; in the meantime talk to people out there. I'll have to call Ron the owner about this, to do damage control. I am really sorry about Dave, but I have to cover our asses too, you understand?"

"Absolutely" Borneo replied. "Could you, as manager, go out and pave the way for us to talk to folks out there? We don't want to panic anyone but there's still a murderer on the loose."

"Sure, but first let me pull his file."

"Mike, you go talk to the bartender, bouncer and wait staff." Lissa suggested.

Petra held up Dave's file. "If anyone fails to cooperate," she said in a harsh tone, "tell them I will dock hours and seize tips."

Lissa gave Petra a look.

"What?" demanded Petra, "Money does talk; don't think it doesn't! I pay better than most managers, I expect absolute loyalty. Call me a bitch, but Dave was one of us. I treat all my talent that way. Ron would agree."

Mike left to go talk to staff, while Lissa collected the information from Petra.

"How is Vincent these days?" Petra asked the young officer. "Is he seeing anyone?"

"Detective Vetters is too busy with his head in his work. He doesn't have a life, but needs one seriously."

"Ah that Vinnie, nothing's changed. Phil has all the fun doing his shtick Tell him if he needs a break, to call me. I'll gladly buy him a round."

Lissa laughed, "Pardon me for seeming slow, but did you and Vetters have a fling?"

"Yeah, but repeat that and I deny everything." Petra winked. "Whatever happens here …?"

"It isn't Vegas but you **have my back Ms. James.**   Thanks for cooperating"

"It's Petra," and she held out her hand. "Here take two comp tickets."

"Wow, thanks!" Lissa said fanning herself with the tickets.

"None needed, just catch the asshole that killed Dave. Say hi to Vince for me."

"Will do, I got a job to do. I have to call the victim's address into Vetters and Swift."

Petra and Lissa left the office to go question the customers.

CHAPTER 3

Vince was sitting at his desk in the squad room when the phone rang. It was Lissa with the details about the dead guy's next of kin. He took down the address, thanked her and hung up.

"Hey Swifty", he bellowed across the room. "We got next of kin, time to do the death call."

"God I hate this part of the job!" Myra said, half to herself and half to Vince.

"It's   worse   that   witnessing   autopsies."
"Much. Dealing with the dead is so much easier, than the ones left behind. Mind you, the smell isn't as bad," she stood up, grabbed her suit jacket and followed Vince out of the station house.

"Shitty, but true, let's get this done."

"Our Vic left a wife behind. Fortunately, there were no kids."

The detectives noticed the house that the late Dave Feener lived in, a wartime bungalow that needed paint with a lawn in disarray.

Vince and Myra pulled up to the house. They proceeded to

the front door, and rang the bell. A young woman, about thirty, answered the door.

Vetters flashed his badge, as did Myra.

"Can I help you?" The young woman asked, puzzled.

"We need to talk. Are you Deborah Feener?"

"Yes, what's this about? Did something happen to Dave?"

"May we come in?"

"Yes, of course," Debbie replied, "sorry for being rude."

Deb let the two detectives into the room and motioned to the couch, and she took the chair facing them.

"So what's going on?" she asked them, "What happened to Dave?" Deb was starting to look frazzled, and naturally so.

Myra looked at Vince, and decided she would handle this. She moved to sit on the coffee table and took Deborah's hand, "I am so sorry Mrs. Feener, and this is not easy. I am afraid Dave has been killed." Myra squeezed, and Deborah looked at her and fell apart.

"What? How? Where? Was it an accident?" She was fighting to retain her composure, but was failing miserably. Tears ran down her face and her chin had started to quiver at the news.

Myra wished it was that simple. "No I am afraid not. He was the victim of a stabbing. He was found by a derelict in the alley behind the Laff Attak.

"It wasn't a robbery. The killer left his ring and his ID. Did Dave have anyone who was mad enough to kill him?"

"Oh fuck," said Deb, "I don't know how many times I told him that shortcut was not safe and no I don't think any one was mad enough to kill him.

"I am not saying he deserved it, by any means. He's everything to me, and now he's gone."

Deborah put her head in her hands and sobbed.

"It's okay Mrs. Feener", said Myra soothingly, "I think I'd react the same way. You're in shock." She looked back at Vetters, and asked for the throw off the back of the couch. Vince passed it to her. He handed it to Myra, she was better at this shit than he was.

"Did he die instantly?"

"Yes, I'm sorry, he didn't have a chance." This was Myra's response.

"Can I see him?"

"Sorry but in the case of a homicide, we have to do an autopsy. I don't think you would want to remember him the way he looks now."

"Then when? I need to see if it's really him. I trust you and all that but I just have to see for myself. You know?"

Myra nodded. "We'll let you know. You can come and pick up his things when we get done with them."

"Is there any one who can stay with you?" asked Vetters.

"My Mom lives down the street, I can call her. This is her house. Dave and I rent it from her and she lives with my Grandma."

"We'll stay until she gets here." Myra was quick to reply.

"I have to call Dave's parents. This is going to kill them."

"They wanted him to go to college. He started but that wasn't enough. He was determined to make it big. The next Robin Williams; he always dreamed about that."

"I can relate, "Vetters told Deb, "My brother Phil is a comic. He grew up watching tapes of all the greats, the family got sick of back to back 'Evening at the Improv'."

"I can't believe how calm I am being."

"It's shock." Myra told her, "We're very sorry this happened to Dave. Petra at the Laff Attak sends her condolences. She said she'd call you in a few days."

"Great, well I better call my Mom. She'll have to call Dave's folks. I can't do it."

Myra put her hands on Debs shoulders. "You need to take care of you, too."

"I know. I loved my husband he was the greatest, but he was

a wee bit impractical. Just do me a favor and get the little shit that did this."

"We are going to do our best."

Deb called her Mom. Minutes later, she and the grandma showed up. The detectives left.

Vince reached out and grabbed Myra in a hug, and kissed her on the side of the head.

"You were great."

"Thanks, but please don't kiss me again, or I'll have to take you down."

"You wound me to the core Swifty." Vetters laughed.

"Yeah, come on I'll buy you a coffee. We have to do the paper work on this one."

CHAPTER 4

Borneo and Lissa were driving back to the precinct, from the Laff Attak. Borneo was singing a bad version of Baba O'Riley.

"Out here in the field, I fight for my meals. I put my back into my livin'

I don't need to fight, to prove I'm right. I don't need to be forgiven."

"Mike, please stop. Good thing you're too old for American Idol. Simon Cowell would have a field day with you."

"Lissa, you wound me deeply. Here I thought I had your back."

"You do, out there, Lissa replied. In here, it's every cop for themselves."

"Look, Mike said; what we found in the alleyway was nasty. I sing to erase the bad memory."

"I understand, but in the meantime you're wrecking my hearing and my sanity."

"Funny girl; you might wanna audition as a comic."

"No not me, that profession might just get me killed."

"I don't think that was the reason for killing the dude. I think the poor fool was just caught in the wrong place at the wrong time."

"What about the program from the club found next to the body from the club he was performing at?"

"We don't get paid to speculate, Lissa; that's the D's job."

"Yeah; she replied, another year of this shit, I am going for the sergeant's badge."

"Great ambition Lissa, good luck with that. I mean that sincerely. You'd do well."

"I don't plan to do the squad car rally for the next thirty years. I know being out there in the field, it's not pretty but it's more exiting than traffic detail."

Borneo had to agree with this, and went on humming anyway to erase the death scene from his head just the same.

He didn't envy the Detectives the nasty job of informing the next of kin. He hated the picture of some officer telling his wife that he may not come home one night. Poor Dave, the unfortunate bastard hadn't seen it coming. There went his shot at fame; thanks to a random ass-hole with a knife.

"Hey, said Lissa. I just remembered something. Petra James, at the Club comp'd us two tickets to come in and see her talent.

"Cool why don't you take a boyfriend? Comedy clubs are great date places."

"And you would know this, how?" Lissa ribbed him.

"Back in the day I used to take the missus to YUK YUKs. She loved it. She said she knew she wanted me after I proved I had a sense of humor."

"How's that?"

"I'm still married to her."

Lissa laughed. "Maybe you should be a comic."

"No, I think I need to be canonized."

This made Lissa howl with laughter.

Chapter 5

It was Saturday at Comic f/x. The Clubs big night of the week; there was a cover charge of $10 at the door and a three drink minimum. It was the place to be on a Saturday. Then again, of course, Ron's Laff attak across town boasted the same. There was no animosity between the two Clubs. Business was business, and the two owners were long time buddies and fellow former comedians.

Jeff had Shelley doing the opening, and Phil doing the anchor act. Jeff felt it was a great pairing and that the two complimented each others style nicely. Shelley had started off with a bang, and would go places with her act. Phil was the consummate professional, and Shelley studied him to get the timing down, she even picked when Jeff referred to what was left of Phil's brain. To which Phil replied a resounding "Fuck you Beals!" Shelley thought Jeff and Phil were great friends despite the low brow banter of the two men. It was true, they were. Shelley, at first hesitated to use fowl language in her act, as momma was prone to come in and see her perform. Jeff told her dirty language was expected in a bar setting and "Yo momma" better adjust her sensitivity level or just stay home. He had said that if she had really raised a family of apes, a little swearing wouldn't kill her. Shelley had to agree with this logic. After all she was for ever telling the boys to get their heads out of their asses and man up.

Shelley was sitting at one of the side tables reading the newspaper when she came across the article involving the young comics' tragic murder the night before. Jeff came over with a coke and a bottle of water for Shelley.

"Thanks for the water. This is just awful, she said pointing at the paper. I knew him. We auditioned together for a job at the Shak. He got it and I came over here.

" I'm glad they took him over you."

"You are?" Shelley replied.

"Yep, I think I got the better comic."

"Really, that's sweet.

"Don't let it go to your head sweet cheeks. I don't need a Diva on my hands. Next thing you'll want is a private masseuse and champagne in your dressing room."

Shelley elbowed him. "You can do that? She joked.

Jeff winked at her. "Why do you think I can pay you so well?"

Shelley cupped her chin in her hands, and looked at him. "Why?"

"Three reasons; One: No Perks. Two: The staff would think I was 'doing' you, and Three: Phil would think I was doing you, and want the same thing. Honey, this mans door don't swing that way."

At this point Phil walked by, and cuffed Jeff upside the head. "Amen to that you perverted A-hole." Phil returned to the table, hopped up on the stool and joined them.

This brought uproarious laughter from Shelley.

However, the three sobered up quickly and once again thought of Dave Feener, who would never get the chance to laugh again, or make anyone else laugh for that matter.   Still sucks about the young guy. Jeff mentioned.

"Yeah, said Phil. My brother's precinct caught this one. Vince said it was ugly.

He told me they found a program for The Shak, by the body."

This is gonna mean bad business for poor Ron. If word gets out a killer saw Dave perform there, follow him out and take him down, no one is going to want to work there.

"Quit the fear mongering Phil." Jeff nodded toward Shelley.

Shelley caught it.

"What are you idiots talking about? She said pointing at the paper. This was just a random act. I am not going to let this scare me."

"It very well might be Shell, but we can't be sure. In the meantime I think I should drive you home tonight."

"It's not necessary, I can handle myself. I will let you guys walk me to my car though and then walk each other back in here.

Jeff sighed. "Is that your final answer?"

"Yes, now, you Mr. Boss man get your ass on stage and introduce the hottest female act in Metro."

"Damn you're a bossy woman. Yo momma would be proud."

"She's good, replied Phil and right about the hot part."

Jeff whacked Phil and told him to get his brain out of his pants, and that he had a wife and two adorable kids.

Shelley put all thoughts of poor Dave out of her head and psyched up for her set. She was looking forward to tonight, as she had some fresh material.

Hey all, everyone got enough to eat and drink, or has our venerable barkeep been hording the peanuts again?

Heard he has to eat breakie standing up. A veDeniseble bachelor breakfast; Lost the kitchen table in the divorce settlement. Said his wife wanted it as a memento from their early days, when they were still having kitchen sex. Last time Wally got any, was in court, when her lawyer screwed him.

The audience loved it when the Comics took cheap shots at the bartender. Wally really didn't min. He couldn't do it but he still got his five minutes of fame just being mentioned in an act. These guys were great.

Seriously I know what its like to have a relationship go south. Thankfully I was the one with the tickets to Hawaii. Last time I saw my ex, he was kissing the Cod down east. The fish didn't look any more impressed with his lip work than I was.

A few titters at this one from the floor.

You get used to doing for yourself again after you kick his sorry ass out the door. Then again I did everything anyway. Now, you know the signs of who really wears the pants in the family when he calls you to fix the plumbing. I like to think I am a liberated woman. I paid all the bills, set the mouse traps and listened to him whine about how inhumane mousetraps really are, and complained that the cheese was too big. The mousie might choke. He quit whining when I said I could find something smaller and pointed at his mid section. Guys get so antsy when you threaten the crown jewels. To his credit he was great in bed, he could snore for hours.

There were groans from the men accompanied by wives or girlfriends who could relate to serial snoring.

Mr. Right and I never really did get married. We were engaged sure, but when I came home one day to find him trying on the contents of my lingerie drawer, I figured he wasn't the girl for me. I can't believe he looked better in it than I did.

I called off the wedding on the grounds that there was only room for one diva per household and I had squatters' rights. He's still pissed that I kept the Chorus line CD.

Now I have no one to fight with over the bathroom in the morning. I can walk around naked if I want to and he's not around to use my Nair. He was slothful and lazy, never got up on time to shave before work. I heard him screaming in agony one morning only to realize he'd picked up my depilatory cream instead of his Gillette

Foamy. He had not only burned his mustache off but managed to exfoliate at the same time. Well good night all, been a slice.

Shelley got off stage to the uproarious laughter of both men and women in the audience. It was a big risk to do jokes about a mans sexual orientation. Her ex, Hank wasn't really gay, but making like he was in her routine was great revenge for the aggravation he caused her during the 6 months in hell. The only reason she stayed so long was to collect good material for her routine.

As she approached the bar, an inebriated customer, grabbed her arm and offered to show her what a 'real man' could do for her in the sack.

She shoved him and replied that he had better unhand her before she shoved his 'nuts' up his nose and she wasn't referring to the peanuts Wally served.

Besides I have a real man at home. He doesn't snore, steal covers, and Bruno respects me in the morning right after I take him for a walk.

The customer spat at her, and called her a few words she had yet to hear in her expanding vocabulary and made a mental note to try them in her routine

At this point one of the bouncers came to her aid.

Jeff came to her side. "Who's Bruno?"

"My Chihuahua; don't piss him off. He bites."

"Heard and noted. Want a drink, now that the sets over?"

"Nah, no alcohol and I really have to get home and walk the wee beastie.

Jeff agreed to walk her to her car and made sure she got in okay; checked the backseat for bogeymen. Shelley cranked her window down and they chatted some.

He gets pissy if I leave him too long. It's great having a dog, but he whines as much as Hank did. "

Jeff laughed. You can tell me about Hank, and I'll tell you about Rita

"The wife?"

"Yeah, Mrs. Beals number one. She gave true meaning to the term Hell on wheels.

"There was more than one?"

Three altogether, Guys in my line of work, Comedy Clubbers as a whole, can't hold on to women too well."

"She didn't last long enough for me to realize what a gold-digger she would have been, had I had any money which was going to pay off the first bitch.

"Number three?" Shelley was curious enough yet afraid to ask.

Jeff went silent. Shelley sensed that this was the one that got away, and he didn't want her to.

"It's late, you sure you don't want me to follow you home?"

"I'm sure. I would feel obliged to serve you coffee, while I let Bruno water my garden, and I don't have any."

"Point taken." Jeff knew when to stop pushing. Besides he had a truckload of accounts to settle for the end of the month. "Night Shell "and he patted her arm. He loved women, in general but after Denise had died on him, he vowed no more women or serious relationships.

Shelley said good night and started up the SUV as Jeff stood and watched her go. Shell was a good one, but no way, she was just too good for him.

CHAPTER 6

Phil Vetters sat in the diner, waiting for his brother Vince to show up. Vince was the detective in charge of the recent murder of Dave Feener. Phil was thinking of the young comedian who had been murdered. He felt for the kid. What a loss. Dave had a marketable talent, but was sadly cut down way too soon. Phil would give everything he had to go five minutes with the killer.

Vince was late, as usual. Phil couldn't wait too much longer as he had a date with Peggy, his wife, before his gig at the club. Phil spent a lot of time on the road as a comic, or late nights at Clubs. Peg used to come and watch him and reveled in his humor. Since the kids came along there was never enough time or money for her to come out. So, as a consolation, Phil would spend an afternoon with her twice a week to have some quality time over lunch or whatever to keep the romance alive. Peg loved hearing his material and gave him ideas for his acts based on time with the kids the pets etc. He did a lot of family related humor now that he was a parent. That's what age did to a comic; took the bite right out of your act. Tonight was Saturday; the night he did his "dumb ass married to a redneck woman act" - a bar favorite. Phil had done this in the days just after he married

Peg. His first two wives had kicked him to the curb for being a two timing idiot. He loved it but, lately he found himself lacking in comparison with the new girl, Shelley. Shelley had an edge, brightness and most of all the hunger to do well. *Maybe I am just losing it. I can't compete with the likes of Shelley and Dave. Maybe one day I'll be the victim of someone with a knife who thinks I no longer have the right stuff. It wouldn't be long before Shelley got the headlining spot if he didn't get his shit together.*

Phil couldn't afford to think this way. Comedy was in his blood ever since high school. One of his buddies had dared him to get on stage for a talent show. He got up and did a few impressions, gagged on the history teachers, and the crowd loved him. From there, he tried out for open mike nights. He was voted class clown. Phil was bitten. His family thought he was nuts to pursue such an impractical career and Dad had threatened to cut him off unless he toed the lined and did the college life. Vince and his sisters felt for him. They knew he had a special talent that they lacked and told him to go for it. This was backed up with get a day job to help with the bills but go ahead and live the dream.

Vince still went to see his shows, but the girls had families, and just couldn't get away. Their parents didn't go. Dad just didn't believe anything would ever come of it and refused to support a useless career. Comedy is hard, it sounds so cliché but it's true. You have to be on a lot of the time and studying life the rest in order to get fresh bits and make sure they weren't someone else's bits first.. Stealing someone's jokes was verboten and killed credibility that you could write your own act. Thus, some days being hilariously funny was more of a chore.

Vince must have got caught up in something, and Peg wasn't gonna show. Phil stood up left his money and tip on the table. He ran across the street to the club in time to go on. Phil headed for the stage to do his first act of the night. After twenty years of doing the dumb ass shtick he was still getting laughs.

Woohoo, and welcome to Comic flx. It's great to see everyone out and getting juiced up. Just a reminder; don't drive home, if you have had too much.

Some women look pretty good after three beers. But there is not a woman out there who looks good at two a.m. haulin' your sorry ass out of jail. In fact, by that point you're back to square one, because she's down right fucking ugly at this point. It kinda negates the purpose of the beer you just consumed.

So, if you're planning to go home to a pretty woman and get laid, leave your keys with Wally behind the bar. He'll drive you home. He's not getting any lately, anyway.

Wally was flipping his middle finger at Phil. The audience was really eating it up, as poor Wally was the brunt of many jokes by comics working at the club.

So I am on my 3rd marriage right now. The first two nailed me for adultery. A word to the wise; men, if you say you're going fishing late at night for mud cat. You'd better be able to produce the fish in question, or at least remove the caught fresh daily sticker off its ass.

*Don't let the little woman or her friends catch you at the legion close to last call, makin' it with the bait and tackle girl. For Pete's sake and better yet, your own; dumb excuses like "But honey, she was showing me her lures! Those just don't work where we lived. Betty's lures had little to do with any kind of fishing. They came big enough to fill a 42DD cup. The DD standing for Double Dang you is in deep shit now boy!!!! Don't be looking to see **any** booty for about a week.*

*This is what I get for marrying a redneck woman. I should have known the marriage was going south when I found her in the back parking lot at our wedding reception. She was beating the snot out of her little brother Bubba J for three timing her attendants, Becky Wanda and Leona. Bubba W (the older brother) was waiting in line to get his ass whooped for the same thing. Remember this, guys. Rednecks are stupid, Redneck women are **smart** and **mean**. Her Bridesmaids, Becky, Wanda and Leona were taking bets and raised enough money to pay for a week at a fishing camp for our honeymoon.*

Betty, wife #2; you remember Little Miss Bait & Tackle? She caught me in my bass boat—(her wedding gift to me), with her sister Bertha Lee. Bertha's only a C cup, but she had skills; her breast size didn't matter. I have to wonder how I ended up in the same mess, must have been drinkin' more than thinkin'. The next thing I am sayin' is "But honey Bertha was just showing me her best fly fishing technique!" How the hell did I know fly fishing had nothing to do with bass boats?

Well, let's just say the judge awarded her a healthy sum of money, and my boat. The judge said any moron who knew that little about fishing didn't deserve a boat.

So now I am a standup comic, married to a woman, whose daddy sells hunting rifles! My sense of humor is the only thing keeping me married and still alive. Just have to be sure and steer clear of the cutie behind the ammunition counter.

Thanks and come again for more life skills from the backwoods! I better get home before the wife meets me at the door with my hunting rifle.

Phil got off stage to a standing ovation. Throughout his routine, the laughter from the floor had been uproarious and people were clapping in appreciation of the truisms being told. That was his best show yet judging by the audience's reaction. City people really ate up the dumb ass routine. He had studied Jeff Foxworthy; the redneck Appalachian jokes really worked for him, so why not use his experiences to his advantage? Even Jeff Foxworthy thought his stuff was funny.

Phil was well and truly stoked after his routine. It had gone so well! No one had heckled him and he was surprised and gratified that the Redneck routine was still popular. Beat the shit out of the cutsie family oriented Pets and Kids shtick. He did need a smoke though.

Phil took the back exit. He really should smoke out front. The last poor SOB that stepped into the alley way for a break got his throat cut. *Ah shit, he thought what are the frigging odds it would happen again? He'd make it a quickie and then go over to the parking garage to get the van and head home to Peg and the kids.*

Phil looked at his watch - 12:30. Damn, getting late. Peg would be getting antsy by now. Dave Feeners death had really freaked her out. God forbid he'd be a statistic of the murder tally in this city. As far as large Edmonton' went; this one didn't have a large homicide rate like some of the others. But having a nice young comic turn up slashed was still enough to freak a guy out. OK Phil, just get your ass home and tear off a piece with the little woman while she is still up and waiting for it.

At 45 he still had a great sex-life with his wife. Other guys he knew were starting to bitch about not getting enough at home and they were looking further afield outside the marriage bed for sufficient action. Not Phil, no sirree. Peg was still gorgeous at 44 as well. No need to look else where for lovin'. It would take him fifteen minutes to walk to the garage to grab the van and another ten to get home.

He was walking briskly as it was a bit chilly, and he felt the hairs standing up at the back of his neck. Phil quickened his pace a bit. He knew there was really no one behind him, but still the memory of the young man's death days before still bothered him. The garage was just up ahead.

He rounded the corner and WHAM - he felt the knife go in and that was it.

CHAPTER 7

"Not funny dude. The redneck shit's been done before find some new material. And now you're a dead man. Maybe in your next life you might find better material." The killer stood up and wiped the blood off the knife and dropped the playbill beside Phil's body. He didn't slash Phil's throat as he had to the other guys. Too much of a repetition would tip the ass-hole cops off to a "serial killer". He wanted to keep the jerks on their toes and chasing their tails. He was a killer - sure - but he was a damn smart one too. Besides, the dead dude was already bleeding out. Time to go find a hiding place and let some poor sucker find the carnage

He knew he was a sick asshole but at the same time loved to have people see his kills. Why do a job when others can't see the fruits of his labors? The playbills were an added feature. If he left one at each scene for a different comedy club, the police would start to chase their damn tails wondering who would be next.

He scrambled to find a hiding place, and found a spot near a van about half way down. Now he could wait for some sucker to discover the carnage. That's why he left his victims out in the open. It caused a shitload of mayhem, and would be the fodder of a few nightmares along the way. It wasn't long before he heard the voices of a young couple entering the garage from the street. Click, click, click, was the sound of a woman's high heels on concrete along with the heavier footfalls of cowboy or construction boots.

3-2-1. Come on honey scream.

"Ah God what the hell Fuck he's dead; quick Alana quick call 9-1-1!"

The girl was shaking. "Yes!" she yelled, "It's a body, dead! Yes very, you idiot get a freaking wagon over here!" The young lady started puking all over her Jimmy Choos. Her boyfriend remained the calm hero. He was comforting his date, as they waited for the police to arrive. Ah! he loved the sound of people losing their dinner after finding his art work. *Time to get the F out of here;* he never stuck around too long to attract attention to himself.

The killer found a way out and walked calmly out of the garage like he had never been there. Just wait 'til the cops found this one.

The first squad cars were showing up and calling for back up as he walked down a back street.

***

Lissa and Borneo were on duty again as the call came in. They were just about to get into the squad car when Vince found them.

"Another DB Lieut." was Lissa's reply to his enquiring look.

"Shit," Vince swore. "What the hell is happening; two in the last three days?"

Lissa proceeded to fill him in on the details. "Eleventh Street Garage; cars are at the scene from what we heard, it's a stabbing: same calling card left. Vic is a male 45, alone. Found by a young couple. Witnesses are still at scene. Crime unit is on route."

"Okay, let's go I'll follow in my car."

"Yes sir." This from Borneo

Lissa looked at Borneo. "Who gets to tell the poor guy it's his brother?"

"I know," said Borneo with regret, "we should have said something. Maybe he shouldn't be involved."

"Think we should call the captain?" Asked Lissa

"And go over Vince's head? He'd have my ass, and you can kiss your sergeant's badge   good-bye."

"If Cappy finds out we didn't go to him," Lissa pointed out, "I may have to kiss it and this one goodbye anyway."

"Okay I'll get Cap and you tell Vince that Phil is dead." Mike replied.

"Screw that –I'll flip you for it."

"Deal," said Borneo as he fished his quarter out.

"Tails," Lissa stated.

It came up tails. Mike swore as he rushed off to deliver the bad news and Lissa picked up the phone.

The captain responded and said that he would talk to Vince at the scene. This was bad. He knew Phil and Vince really well. Normally he would have called anyone else off the case but he trusted Vetters to do the right thing and excuse himself.

***

Borneo caught up to Vince at the police garage. "Lieut. There's something you should know about this one."

"What's that? "

Mike knew no other way but to just say it. "It's your brother sir, it's Phil. I am truly sorry sir.

Vince's face was a blank. "Why apologize? It's not your fault damn it; let's go. Where's your partner?"

"Um" Borneo was clearly stalling, not knowing what he should say next.

"You better be about to tell me she's talking to the Captain."

"Yes as a matter of fact she is."

"Good, our asses are covered. Let's move."

"Do you really think you should be in on this one?"

Vince's tone was emotionless and business like. "Officially, now that I know, I am only going to I.D. the victim as a family member. I have that right. This is the Captains case now. I do want details about the case and I am going to ask to be the one to tell Peg. That's what I am going to tell Cap as well. I will however, take Myra with me."

Lissa caught up to them a minute later with the Captain close behind.

"I'm very sorry about your brother sir." She said sadly.

"Both of you please ram the apologies. I have to go say good-be to my brother."

"Come with me." replied the captain.

"It's Okay. I am fine. I need to go get Myra and then go tell Peg her husband isn't going to make it home. I'll be right behind you."

The Captain nodded. Every one got in their respective vehicles, and headed to the crime scene.

As Vince suspected, it was as grisly as any of the others. Judging by the layout of the victim, it was clearly the work of the same squirrel. "God damn him to hell." Vince uttered under his breath.

Vince pulled himself up short. The captain was right beside him and put his hand on his shoulder.

"Geez Vince. I honestly don't know what to say right now."

"Nothing to say Cap', absolutely nothing—just don't say I am sorry or I'll feel compelled to punch you. I really don't need internal affairs up my ass for that."

"They wouldn't hear it from me. As far as I am concerned you're just here to ID Phil's body."

Myra had shown up at this point and was about to utter an apology for which Borneo, Lissa and the captain all did the signal to not say a word.

"Be strong Vince." We are with you on this one."

Vince nodded and motioned Myra to follow him in her car.

Chapter 3

Vince hated this part of the job with a passion. Moreover, it was going to be especially hard to break the news to Peg. He was dragging Myra into it for two reasons: she was better at it than he was and he was just too close to the situation in this case. Vince was basically just there to support Peg and the kids.

They rang the bell.

"You ready for this Vince?"

"Is anyone ever ready?"

"No, but that's where our sensitivity training comes in handy."

"How true." At this point Peg answered the door.

"Hi Vince", said Peg when she saw it was her brother-in-law, "what brings you here? I thought it was Phil. May he had forgotten his keys again. Funny guy, but he can be a real bonehead."

Peg looked at Vince again, and somehow she just knew it was bad. She wailed and sank to her knees.

"NO not Phil!"

Vince knelt down to grab her.

"Come on hon, let's get you inside." He pretty much carried her to the couch and held her.

"I wanted to be here when Myra broke the news to you," he said gently, "I'm not here in an official capacity due to the circumstances but I didn't want you to be alone. Myra and I still have to tell the parents about Phil. I'll help you explain it to the kids too."

Myra introduced herself at this point. "Mrs. Vetters, my name is Myra. I work with Vince. I just want to begin by saying how sorry I am. I knew Phil and he was a charming and caring man, He loved you very much. He didn't suffer. It was quick."

"Thank you." Said Peg hoarsely. "Was it like the other comic, Mr. Feener? "

"I am afraid so Mrs. Vetters"

"Oh call me Peg." Vince handed his sister-law a tissue. Peg was calming down a bit but he stayed and held her to him.

"Vince can you call Mom and Dad and my parents and get them over here? I don't want to have you repeat this over and over, and I don't think I can do it."

"Good enough," said Vince, nodding, "are you okay for a minute?"

"Go I'll be fine," sighed Peggy, "I'll just chat with Myra here. Now that I know Phil didn't suffer, I'll be okay."

Vince kissed the side of Pegs head and when off to contact the rest of the family.

Myra moved over to the couch and took Peg's hand.

"We are going to find the sicko who did this", she said. "Neither Phil or Mr. Feener deserved to die like that; no one does."

"I hope to hell you do Myra", said Peg bitterly, "Phil and I were supposed to meet for lunch but I got waylaid and couldn't call before he went on tonight. I feel bad. We had words this morning about his job and how it was all fine and well but I needed help with finances. I said he needed and to go get a side job and grow the hell up. I will never get a chance to apologize for my harshness."

"I'm sure Phil understood your frustration."

Vince was back. "Mom and Dad are on their way over. No answer at your folks' house. "Umm where are Will and Patty?"

"At friends; on sleepovers; just as well. I don't think I am able to bring myself to tell them right now." Peg grabbed another tissue and wiped her eyes again.

"I think I should stay here with you tonight," Vince replied.

Minutes later Vince and Phil's parents arrived, and when they saw Myra and Peg's tear stained faces, immediately surmised that the situation was not good. This brought on more crying from mom and dad. Vince managed to hold it together for the sake of his family. Myra felt comfortable enough to leave and let the family of her close friend and co-worker grieving their loss. Vince walked her to her car. He offered his thanks for handling that and he would call in the morning. Myra waved and drove off as Vince felt the first tears of the night come to the surface.

***

The morning after he and Myra delivered the bad news to Peg, Vince hit a liquor store for a mickey of Johnny Walker. He rarely drank but this called for it. Vince knew the autopsy was today and wanted to observe. He also knew that they probably wouldn't let him watch as it was Phil. It wasn't like he really wanted to see Phil's insides –not a pretty sight – hell, Phil wasn't pretty on the outside on the best of days - still he thought he should be there.

Captain Shaw and ME Bruce Watters were in the autopsy suite along with Myra. Vince walked in and they all looked at him.

Captain Shaw approached Vince.

"You really can't be here my friend and we both know it." The Captain had his hand on Vince's shoulder.

"Yeah I know, but I had to see him."

"Trust me Vince; this is the part of Phil you really don't want to see. Besides I can smell ya clear across the room. Go home, take a shower and sleep; seriously now!"

Vince knew his boss was right, so he turned around and headed out of the suite. He had to get some rest and then be over at Peg's so they could start the process of dealing with funeral arrangements with her and the folks.

He could have gotten pissed off and insisted on staying, but what good would that do; other than getting written up.

Home he went to sleep off the pain of his brothers' brutal murder, with a vow of revenge on the son of a bitch who did it.

CHAPTER 9

Despite the Police's best efforts to keep the murders of Dave Feener and Phil Vetters out of the media, the newshounds had gotten a hold of the juicy tidbits of the cases. The public was now screeching about a serial killer out there. The police chief held a press conference stating that while the two murders were alike in many ways, it did not mean that there was a serial killer loose, and that the media should quit with the fear mongering.

Morale at Comic F/X and at the Laff Attak was at an all time low. There was irony for you. The two places in town where a person could go have a few giggles were dark; especially at Comic F/X, where Jeff had gathered the staff together to deliver the news of Phil's death. It was the worst news he had ever had to give at work. Firing people was a piece of cake next to this.

"So what's next?" said a waitress in the back. "Do we just shut down until the asshole is caught? If we have to I am screwed!" Cindy was in tears. "I need the F'ing job."

"Quit whining Cindy", said Dan dismissively, "Phil's wife doesn't have a husband anymore, and you are worried about your stupid—assed waitress job."

Cindy shot her co worker Dan the finger at this comment.

Jeff shushed them both and told them to axe the bickering.

To Cindy's question he simply answered that they would not shut down and give the killer the idea that he had won. Phil would not have wanted them to cave in.

"Phil's brother Vince has assured us that the police are going to work day and night to find the perp who did both victims," Jeff assured his staff, "he can't officially work the case under the circumstances, but he is willing to come over here and be security pro bono; of course this is completely off the record. But watch for any suspicious behavior at the shows. We have to show the city and everyone out there it's business as usual. Safety precautions will be taken 'til the case is closed. There will be paid cab rides from door to door or you can buddy-up getting home. Bottom line no one leaves here alone. Everyone clear on this?"

All staff nodded. Lists were made as to car pooling based on proximity.

Shelley stood up. "Let's give a show of strength in Phil's memory," she declared, "Jeff and I have been talking with Ron over at the Laff attak. All the comics in the area and a few of the bigger names are going to come together to do a benefit to raise money for the widows and any dependants of the two dead men. I think Phil and Dave would appreciate this."

The staff gave a cheer and a round of applause. Details needed to be ironed out about the benefit; meanwhile both clubs would operate business as usual. Similar security measures were taken at The Laff attak as at Comic f/x. Shelley, although she felt she was stepping on a man's grave, had agreed to take the headlining spot even though jokes were the last thing on her mind. No one felt like laughing, but all the shit about the show going on for the two dead guys was true. A troop of newbies were being auditioned to take her spot. The next few days were going to be hell as far as hours were concerned. Shell just wanted to go home and sleep but knew Jeff needed and wanted her help in picking a new crop of comics. Ones she hoped would not be meeting the knife if the sicko wasn't caught soon. She was waiting for Jeff to finish up, as he had offered, no insisted on being the one to drive her home. If there was anyone she wanted to escort her to the door it was definitely her boss.

The car was silent as Jeff drove to the west end where Shell lived. Neither one of them wanted to express their sorrow for their friends' death. It hurt too much to talk about. The funeral had come and gone after the body had been released. It had given Vince's family some closure but the real healing would not begin until the squirrel responsible was behind bars.

Shelley spoke up. "Want to come in for coffee? I really don't want to be alone. I am dead tired, but Phil's death really got to me."

"Sure." Jeff said taking the house key and letting them both in.

The dog greeted them at the door. Jeff put him in the yard as Shelley started getting the coffee together. Once the pooch's needs were attended to, Jeff helped her with the refreshments. Shelley was just putting the cream away when Jeff stopped her in front of the fridge. He started to massage her shoulders remarking that she was tense. Shelley moaned in sheer appreciation of having someone to give her this much attention. The affection well had long gone dry even before she and the boyfriend had split. It was nice to see there were still men around who didn't pull the captain caveman role. Jeff stopped rubbing her shoulders; turning his attention to her neck. He began stroking it with feather like touches that sent quivers up the back of her legs and spine. He leaned in close, kissing her neck and earlobes.

"Oh god that is so hot! Whatever you do, don't let your conscience step in and say how wrong this is."

"This is wrong?"

"This is oh-so-you are my boss -wrong." Shelley replied breathlessly.

Jeff stopped in mid nibble. "No one needs to know and I won't get sued for sexual harassment will I?"

"Not on your life." Shelley turned around and kissed him

deeply. She then directed his hand toward her blouse where he started undoing the buttons. She unbelted his pants and stripped off his shirt. Her blouse drifted to the floor and she felt Jeff caressing her breasts through the fabric of her bra.

"Ah keep it up and I will never let you go home." She moaned.

"Really, is that so?" Jeff stopped her. "If that's all it takes I would have tried this weeks ago."

As he was talking, he found the dainty clasp of her lacy bra and released her velvet breasts, caressing her nipples.

Shelley couldn't take much more as she removed her skirt and stepped out of it. She was wearing scanty hose and her heels along with a blue satin thong. Jeff, too was standing in his boxers and Shelley slowly edged the waistband over his hips, releasing what she thought was one of the most glorious examples of manhood she had ever feasted her eyes upon.

She stopped short, taking it all in.

"What is wrong? Don't tell me you have changed your mind."

"Oh no, that's not the problem."

"So what is?" Jeff looked confused.

"It's nothing really. Just tell me you will respect me after this —It's safe to say at this point there is no going back to a strictly platonic thing. I am about to make you forget I work for you. It's too early for the L word but respect is important to me." Shelley tried to sound reassuring.

"Honey, I respected you when I saw you cut Gordo down to size in the middle of your act. I wanted you instantly but I needed a comic more at that point. Now shut up and kiss me before I remember who I am and fire your sexy little ass."

They both laughed as they slid to the floor to pay mutual respect to each others' finer points.

After the greatest sex Shelley had had in a very long time. She lay beside Jeff panting and spent but sated.

"Wow," was all she could muster, "I can't remember the last time I did that and didn't have to fake it."

Jeff laughed. "Thanks, I think."

"It's not that, you were fantastic." She planted an appreciative kiss, on his shoulder. "However I don't relish sleeping on the kitchen floor." Shelley got up and saw Bruno standing on his hind legs waiting to be let in. "Oops we forgot someone."

Jeff was putting on his boxers, and then went over to let the dog in.

Shelley fed the little guy, and led Jeff to her room.

Chapter 10

The killer sat in his lazy-boy and nursed his beer. The news was on and he watched to catch the piece on his two works of art.

The police had nothing on his two latest master-pieces. The very fact that the last murder was the brother of Detective Vetters was a real score. This ought to get the pigs off their asses and let the games begin.

He had caught a glimpse of the bitch at Comic f/x doing her funny thing. As hard as it was to actually admit…she was funny. He was tempted to let her live. However; the fact that she had the cajones to diss him after her act really pissed him off. The only thing he could do at the time was spit at her. He admired her moxie. She had done a fantastic job dressing down Gordo on her first day. He got hard just watching her on stage doing her act. The little tart would have to be roughed up a bit just to show her who was boss.

No woman had ever said no to him when he advanced himself on her. She had broken the rules and would pay for the mistake.

He had seen her the other night, leaving Comic f/x with her manager.

They never had any clue he had followed them to her apartment, another bonus. He even got to see the half time show in the kitchen while the little mutt was pissing up a tree –shame on them for making the little fart wait and freeze his Willy while they did the horizontal mambo on her linoleum. If he was going to have his way with her, then he would have to be disposed of. There was only room for one boss in that bitch's life.

If it had just been a night of raw sex between the two he wouldn't bother offing the guy. He did, however, suspect there was going to be more to that relationship that met the eye. A clear obstacle to him getting her where she deserved to be—flat on her back and doing his bidding. And then maybe he'd let her live after she had serviced him. And then again maybe not.

Just thinking of screwing her brought him a release he could only imagine in his wildest wet dreams. But what was even more stimulating to him was imagining her lying in a dark alley with a gash in her stomach and a slashed carotid. Maybe he'd make her watch him do her boss for snubbing him that one night. Yep, that sounded good to him: torture her, fuck her and finish her off.

Meanwhile he watched the rest of the nightly newsmen announce that the cops had no leads on the two murders, only that the victims were found slashed with playbills beside them.

They really were a bunch of useless farts.

The next item up was related to the fundraiser being held to help the victim's families. Tickets were $40 a head and the event was to be held at Cormorant Hall in a weeks time.

Woohoo! he thought to himself - a target rich environment! There would be hundreds of allegedly funny people, all in the same place at once; a veritable smorgasbord of potential victims.

He could hardly wait.

CHAPTER 11

Jason Tyler was waiting in line in front of Comic f/x with all the other wannabes. There had been a general call go out through the agency he used. After Phil Vetters untimely and grisly demise, the Fix was filling the spot the dead man had occupied, and Jason wanted it. He wanted it so bad it left a taste in his mouth and a hunger in his belly. Finally, at the age of 32, after slinging Chinese food around town, doing dishes between deliveries and washing people's dirty jockeys at his day job, he was ready to tell old Chong Fin where to shove his chicken balls. The job Jason was actually applying for was Shelley Morgan's job, and Shelley was taking Phil's place as she had seniority so to speak. That was good enough for him; any spot at the Fix was good as long it was on stage.

As Jason waited, the front door of the club opened, and a short stocky guy with a bad attitude was summarily removed from the club by a big beefy looking bouncer. The little dude was clearly not happy as he was shouting four lettered epithets at the bigger man. "You big hairy mother, don't you know who I am?" he said in a huff with his hands on his hips.

The bouncer was not impressed. "Listen pipsqueak I don't

frigging care if you're the tooth fairy. They said they would call you if they wanted you, now toddle off and do whatever it is you do for a day job."

"Well I never!" The shorter one of the two huffed.

The bouncer suggested he start whatever it was he never did.

" 'The Ant' doesn't take this sort of crap laying down you know!" declared the little dude.

The bouncer folded his arms. "Ants usually get stepped on where I come from. So get going before I eat you for breakfast!"

The Ant retorted with a "Bite me Honey!" and flipped the bird as he walked away, still cursing.

Jason and the others in line watched the exchange and clapped as the bouncer announced the next hopeful.

"Is there a Jason Tyler in line?"

Jason was brought out of his reverie –"That's me!!!!!!!"

The bouncer looked at the form Jason held out to him and handed it back.

"Give this to Jeff, Shelley and Wally. You have 5 minutes to show 'em what you have. Do your best; the judges don't bite. Just don't go all Hollywood on them like our little friend back there. Between you and me he's not getting hired. Not 'cos he's not talented –in fact he is pretty damned hilarious but he copped an attitude when they didn't hire the little diva on the spot."

"Thanks, replied Jason has he headed to the main bar."

The bouncer nodded and gave him the thumbs up sign.

Jason approached the panel and shook hands and introduced himself.

Jeff stated who he was and introduced Shelley as one of his fellow judges and Wally as the bartender who had a great ear for a good laugh, and had heard every redneck joke north of the Mason-Dixon Line and every Yankee joke below it.

"You have 5 minutes to knock my socks off; Shelley's thong is off limits and Wally goes commando so don't bother. If we like you, you have 15 minutes one night this week to test your mettle in front of live people."

Jason got up on stage and delivered the best he had.

Hey every one, how are the drinks. Hope Wally hasn't been watering down the rum on ya. You'd think that with a five dollar cover charge they could afford to make better drinks.

Anyways, my name is Jay I am 32, I live here in town with my girlfriend and two pet snakes.

The judges were chucking and making notes as Jay did his bit.

The snakes are hers. Not quite sure of her motivation there; maybe it's to keep me in line sexually speaking. You know—perform well or else. One has to have a really good sense of his prowess in bed with two two-foot long and 3 inch thick boas lying around. Are these guys there as a visible threat to the manhood or just to show me there is longer and thicker to be had?

I have two jobs to keep food on the table. One is slinging Chop Suey seven nights a week at an all you can eat buffet. The owner keeps asking me to go hunt down stray animals between deliveries. I deliver the stuff and do dishes. I get a lot of abuse on the delivery end of things. I have been called a mother so often I am starting to expect cards and flowers every year. Shelley was laughing out loud at this joke.

My other job is washing and folding other people's clothes at the local Laundromat. Imagine the fantasies that can arise while folding someone's thong only to have it crushed when some large woman named Bertha comes to claim the laundry later on. I often even find lost panties in the dryers. The silk bikinis are great, it's the huge granny pants that would fit a line backer I can really do without. The other part of my job includes cleaning the washers and dryers between uses —looking for loose change—so basically I am a glorified panhandler.

Jeff gave his time's up signal

"Very good," was Jeff's analysis, "can you come back tonight with ½ hrs worth of stuff?"

"Hell yeah!!!!!!!!!!!! What time?"

"8.30?"

"I'll be here—unless the slasher has other plans."

Jeff and Shelley scowled. "No slasher humor dude," said Jeff sternly, "Phil was a friend."

Jason cringed at his own *faux pas*. "Shit, sorry I forgot, won't happen again.

Jeff nodded his acceptance. "That reminds me," He said, "we are having a benefit to collect money for Phil's family and that of Dave Feener, the first victim. Care to take part? Good cause, and it might get you further exposure in the biz?"

"Sure Jeff, I would love to help out as long as I can keep my foot out of my mouth."

"No worries guy. It's just that it's so soon after his death so we are still a little raw over losing Phil."

"Deal. Well I will see you at 8:30 –I have what I just gave you and a few other bits I want to put together and practice."

Shelley looked at him and replied that he was a shoe-in for the job.

Jason left the club feeling like a lion after a fresh kill.

He was stoked that he would be performing at an actual club that night. He was indeed a happy guy. However until he made it big he still had to fold other peoples jockey shorts. There were always bills to pay, and now with the wedding and a baby coming along that was all the more important. His writer friend Camille and her husband Sean at the Laundromat would be happy to know he had finally caught a break. Maybe Camille could help him write a killer routine for the benefit. It was a good thing tonight was a night off from the Chow Mein Hut. Meanwhile he still had to go in and clean the machines before going on.

***

The killer saw the young man leave the comedy club. The guy just looked too happy; must mean that he got a job there. He'd have to pay a visit to Comic F/X to check out the new talent. Maybe someone really bad would show up and he'd be ready to remedy the situation. Some people in this world didn't have the talent to suck their own thumbs, let alone get up on stage and make people laugh. He knew he was funny. Unfortunately there were people out there who couldn't spot talent if it bit them in the ass. In truth he really should be going after the so-called talent scouts and club owners and not the hapless fools they give the breaks to. Who were they trying to fool really, the public or the wannabes begging for jobs?

He was bold enough to walk up to the board posted outside the club that was advertising the up-coming fundraiser for the deceased family members.

Well, isn't that nice. Someone is taking care of the families of his victims. It is very heart warming to see that someone was taking the time to care for the ones left behind due to my handy work. There are going to be quite a few potential victims at that event. Oh well, their time will come to meet my blades of fury.

It was time to go and sharpen those blades in time for tonight's show.

CHAPTER 12

Jason was ready for his first night on stage. Anticipation was eating him up and he was sucking back the water and the Maalox like there was no tomorrow. Maybe there will be no tomorrow---Nope, don't think like that Jay he thought to himself ---It's a case of kill or be killed, though of course not in the literal sense of the word.

Let's go slay the crowd.

Shelley walked up, and put her hand on Jason's shoulder.

"So big guy, are ya ready yet? Gonna go give the audience shits and giggles?"

"They better giggle or I am going to shit."

"Good one. Don't let the assholes out there get to ya.

"If they start to heckle you laugh along with them. Don't get nasty back. Make it look like you agree with them that you are the hack they think you are. Nothing shuts a heckler up faster is the appearance that their lame comments don't bother you at all. Don't engage a bigger meaner guy in a verbal cat and mouse game. Trust me you are the mouse in that case and the cat will wait outside and trounce your ass after the show. The bouncers can take care of the dude while he is in here. When you get out on that side walk afterwards, you are on your own. Keep in mind also if they are drunk they are apt to be even meaner."

"Gotcha coach," Jason smiled.

"Okay lecture's over," Shelley grinned back at him.

"Great. Thanks Shelley. Hey, can I ask you something?"

"Yeah. What?" Jason might be her age but he reminded her of the kid brother she never had. She felt an instant rapport with him and wanted to help him with his act.

"Do you really think there's a serial killer out there?"

"Well it certainly seems that way; but I am not going to let the idiot scare me out of performing. I refuse to think about it. Don't let the fear get in your way. "

Jason got up on stage after Jeff introduced him as the newest member of the Comic F/X family. He also mentioned that Jason would be taking part in the Comics Relief Fundraiser to take place three weeks time, and that all the cover charges and ticket costs were going to aid the families of fallen comic brethren.

Jason used the same piece as he did for his audition and added some material to bring it up to the full half hour set. He wowed every one from staff to audience. People gave him a standing ovation.

Jason felt great. The fear of making an ass of him onstage wasn't much of an issue any more. He did need another act for the benefit as it was a special occasion. He could talk about pending marriage from a guy's point of view and impending fatherhood. The only fear there was having Christine kick his ass. He wasn't so sure that Chris was really into the comedy thing.

As Chris had the car that night he had taken transit to work but he didn't see a bus coming so he hailed a cab. It just so happened that it was his friend Steve driving. Steve's girlfriend, he knew from the Lamaze classes he and Christine were taking. The girls had bonded over their approaching motherhood. Steve couldn't always go to the classes due to his taxi shifts. Jay and Steve managed to hook up as pals due to the one thing they had in common: both their women were expecting and suffered from food cravings and promised to call each other when they were sent on food gathering missions. They often compared notes on the odd concoctions they had been sent out to get. Now there was good fodder for a comedy routine: the things you get talked into buying but would never eat. He would definitely keep track of Christine's weird menus from now on.

Jay got in the front seat beside Steve and told him he was heading home for the night as Steve started up the cab. "Hey dude how's it hangin'?" asked the driver.

"That's the thing. It's just hanging," replied Jason with a shrug, "she doesn't want it at this stage."

"Mine neither", said Steve. "On top of that she's obsessed with a stand up comedian who whines constantly. Everyday I go home afraid she'd dump me for a good joke."

"It can't be that bad. Christine tells me you're obsessed with eighties music; the decade of one hit wonders and guys with parachute pants and weird hair cuts."

"You got me there. It's not my fault I look like Corey Hart."

"Who?" pondered Jason. "Oh yeah I remember: the sunglasses at night dude. Makes ya wonder why. He either had a heavy substance abuse problem or he was hiding the black eye he sported for coming home late too many nights."

"You should use that for material man; its good stuff", laughed Steve. As he said this they were arriving at Jason's apartment.

"Yeah I kind of need new stuff," said Jason, "this will work."

"Anyway, I better get home to the future Mrs. Tyler before she forgets who I am."

"Hey Jay," called Steve as his friend was getting out of the cab, "call me if you need to escape for a beer one night. I am on all night call on the cell if Chris craves something weird so I can bring it by the house."

Jay gave the cabbie the thumbs up sign and went inside as Steve drove off.

***

Back at Comic F/X the bar was closing. Shelley was waiting for Jeff to finish up the books in the back office. Wally left saying goodnight while Shelley was sitting close by at a table reading the paper. Shelley waved and went back to the paper.

They were still speculating about the comic murders, for which there were as yet no solid leads. There was mention of how the case was stalled because the lead investigator's brother Phil was the latest victim, and so he had been taken off the case. The police didn't want to take any chances that Detective Vetters wouldn't "go postal" on a suspect should they find one.

In Shelley's mind, the media had no faith in the police. But she felt differently; To Shelley it was just a matter of time before the killer would slip up and that would be it. No more fears of being out late alone. Having said that, she loved the time she got to spend with Jeff as a result of him wanting to keep her safe. He had spent the last two weeks since Phil's death driving her home. Afterwards he spent some nights in her bed. Other nights he went over to Peg's to help with the kids. His niece and nephew still had night terrors about a killer taking daddy away; Shelley really felt bad for them. She understood what losing a parent was like. The nature of her father's passing had not been violent but the agony of losing a parent takes a while to get over no matter what the circumstances were.

Well that was enough morose news for one night. Shelley switched over to the comics section to find something light to read while waiting for Jeff to finish up in the office.

She was just reading the last strip when Jeff emerged. He went behind the bar and held up a glass, offering her a night cap. She nodded, moved over to a bar stool and sat down. Jeff poured a gin and tonic for himself and a rum and coke for her.

"Skol." Jeff said while holding up his glass.

"What's the occasion?" She toasted in return.

"To celebrate another fabulous night in the comedy biz. We did well tonight. Both you and Jay slaughtered the audience! Our box office did a record amount of sales. That's a reason to cheer these days. Did you notice any cops here tonight?"

"Not off-hand, no."

"Good, that's the whole point. Vince was hiding in the back row. Called me after the show; loved your bit. He also thinks Jason is a great fit. Well, enough shop talk for now let's just enjoy the peace and quiet and each other."

Jeff and Shelley clinked glasses and he leaned in for a kiss. The kiss deepened and Shelley climbed on onto the bar and wrapped her legs around Jeff's waist. Shelley moaned in pleasure. She reached for the rim of her shirt and pulled it over her head revealing her lace bra.

Jeff whistled at the sight and started to kiss her neck.

"Take your shoes and stockings off."

Shelley did so leaving her skirt on. Jeff tore at his shirt and pulled it over his head and then undid his jeans and let them drop to the floor. Shelley was standing in front of Jeff fingering her way around the waistline of his boxers and yanked, leaving him naked. No words were needed between them as they knew where it was leading. Jeff leaned forward and unclasped Shelley's bra His eyes told her that he wanted her and she nodded. He grabbed her waist and lifted her to give him entry. Shelley sighed and wrapped her arms around his neck. They kissed as Jeff held her to him and made love to her with reckless abandon. The feel of skin against skin as they mated was amazing. Shelley felt the heat rising up from her toes as she climaxed. Jeff followed suit and moaned in sheer pleasure of the experience. It was just what both of them needed.

Jeff finally spoke. "Good God woman. You have skills!!!"

"Well, Shelley offered in return, "you ain't so bad yourself mister."

Shelley was starting to pull her clothes on. "I love you and I hate to screw and run but I just remembered the dog needs out."

"What did you just say?"

"The dog, Jeff, we gotta get the dog."

''No, before the part about the dog. The…."

"I love you Jeff now let's move."

"Okay, that's what I thought." He stopped.

"Shell'?"

"Yeah?"

He looked straight at her. "Love you too Babe."

Shelley smiled. "Great, now if my dog pees on my rug, you're buying me a new one!"

They finished dressing, grabbed their coats and rushed home to take care of her dog.

CHAPTER 13

The killer was watching from across the street as Jeff and Shelley left the club.

Why so late? He wondered. Everyone's gone for the night; yet the boss and the funny lady still there after hours. Maybe there was some extra funny business going on. Well that won't last, if I have any thing to do with it . Jeff will be history after I show Shelley what a real man can do for her. Jeff should be warned that fooling with the employees is a no-no. Well I might let her live long enough to see him croak. Watch her beg for his life, kill him anyway, then slit her pretty little throat. This is after making Jeff watch me have my way with his woman.

Yes, Hank you are a mean son-of-a-bitch. I get to get my ya-yas out and still experience the thrill of a kill. Enjoy her while you can Jeffy-boy. Your days are numbered pal.

The killer wondered if he should just follow them home and do them that night. However he thought better of it. It was best to save the blood bath for the gala performance/fundraiser in a week's time. Patience was a virtue he still had, and he would wait to savor the moment. Mother wouldn't approve of any haste in this matter. Not that mother would really approve of his killing spree either, the point was moot. It was too late in the game to stop while he was on a roll. This was the most fun he had ever had in his forty miserable years. Dear old mom had seen to that. Fun was a sin. Mind you she had enough fun, as it were, flogging him while he lay prostrate before the wooden cross on their living room wall. Yes dear Florrie was a real fanatic and she never let him forget he was headed for hell, no matter what he did. She was saving him by beating the devil out of him. She would make him sit and listen to her say the rosary and Hail Mary's after every beating, while letting his cuts bleed. The miserable bitch kept this up til he was eighteen. He had had enough after years of torture. One day he snapped and caught the old bag by surprise. He laughed as he watched her choke when he strangled her with her own flogger.

After that he didn't have to fear the beatings anymore - but he could still hear her voice condemning him every day. So he killed to drown the voices and get rid of them. Hank didn't believe in hell himself. It was Florrie's belief in the nether world. She made it sound so convincing that what the devil would do to him was much worse than what she was doing. It was later in life that he realized she was full of shit. Coming out of his reverie, the killer decided that indeed waiting for the fundraiser to kill the comics was good enough.

He had to think of a good method of killing in a building full of clowns. Stabbing them one by one wouldn't do, there were too many chances to get caught. Maybe a bomb, or just simply torching the convention center would take care of that many so-called funny people. One thing was for sure though - he was going to have the last laugh. Who said that Hank Cavanaugh didn't kill?

The killer decided there was a time and a place to give Jeff and Shelley their due. He had other things to consider in planning the grand finale. Maybe he would knife a few others before that, who knew? He drove off to his small closet apartment to contemplate his next move and fantasize about Shelley's body under his, writhing with pleasure.

Chapter 14

In the station house at precinct 74, a meeting was being held for the task force put in place to stop the killings and capture the squirrel. Lissa and Borneo were there and along with the other detectives they were waiting for the captain to start proceedings.

There had been a lull in the killings since Phil Vetters' death, however it was too much to hope that they had stopped as suddenly as they had started. The entire police force was on high alert. The word from the Chief was DO NOT CEASE UNTIL HE IS CAUGHT! In other words, don't let the asshole catch us with our pants down.

The captain was running late but that was par for the course. He was a great boss but lacked good time management skills.

Mike Borneo was standing by the coffee machine. The smell of hours old sludge was wafting through the briefing room along with yesterday's Boston creams. Cops, coffee and donuts seemed to go hand in hand and seemed to be the life force of the department. Homicide detectives argued that chocolate donuts and caffeine staved off job related stress. Mike knew from his dietitian that the accumulated cholesterol consumed by police officers would kill several head of cattle. It was coronaries and dying on duty that really cut down the police force in droves. Mike still consumed his fair share of caffeine and sweets despite this fact.

"Good God;" he exclaimed, "doesn't anyone ever replenish the coffee around here? What ever happened to the always fresh- -twenty minute rule?"

"Mike, this isn't Starbucks. We're not getting paid to be baristas!" This was Lissa's comeback.

"Yeah, but this swill isn't fit for pigs." Mike retorted in kind.

"If you think it's swill as you say don't drink it." Lissa was having none of his complaining today.

Mike spotted the department clerk. He handed her a twenty dollar bill and sent her for real coffee from Books & Beans, along with some 'healthy muffins' - which meant they contained trail mix.

The Captain arrived, with Vince right beside him. Medical Examiner Watters was also in attendance.

The Captain began his address. "You all know Vince Vetters? Well for those who don't, he was working this case before the killer nailed his brother. Vince is with the task force in an unofficial capacity. M.E. Watters is also joining our group as he presided over both the autopsies. He will be speaking later in reference to the kind of weapon used and what we should be looking for. Now two deaths doesn't necessarily mean we have a serial killer but we aren't about to push our luck to say the killings are the work of two different people given the layout at the scenes and the fact that both victims were comics. We like the same moron for both crimes.

"I want to lay out how we are going to proceed with the investigation. Several things need to be done to further ensure the safety of any comedians and to the general population of the city.

"First of all: we need officers to go into the clubs. Both the Laff attak and Comic F/X have been targeted by this nut. Your job will be to sit in the back of the club and act like the other club-goers; two Officers per night, per club. If you don't volunteer you will be assigned. The teams will be the same but you will pull duty at both clubs."

Lissa raised her hand and that of Borneo.

"Great! The captain replied. "Our first two volunteers, thanks guys." Soon after more teams were formed and were asked to meet with Vince for how to proceed.

The Captain resumed his talk. "Secondly, and very important to all of us; there will be a fundraiser for both Phil's and Dave's families at The Cormorant Convention Center in two weeks time. Security will be tight. No one without a ticket will be admitted. Uniformed officers will be assigned for duty; however, the already assigned teams will be in the audience and will be activated should a problem arise.

M.E. Watters got up and briefed the group about the weapon used on both deaths. He believed that the same type of knife was used but not the same one. He surmised that the killer had a collection. Watters was no profiler but he had his theories about the killer. Obviously the squirrel had a hate on for comedians and was letting it show.

Soon after that, Vince was going over team assignments and schedules and then the group dispersed.

Lissa informed the Captain that she had tickets for The Laff attak, as provided by Petra.

The Captain raised his eyebrow at this news. Normally this was seen as graft and it was not allowed. In the current circumstance he let it go, and hoped it would not come back to bite him on his ass later.

Myra and Vince would take that night's shift at Comic F/X while Lissa and Borneo were assigned to the Laff attak.

Borneo complained that it was a night off but would take one for the cause. Lissa punched him playfully and thanked him for his 'selfless' act as they headed home to rest up for the evening.

Chapter 15.

Over at Ron's Laff Attak, the evening was just getting started. Lissa and Borneo found corner table which had a full view of the stage, yet was still inconspicuous. The Headliner that night was Suzanne Goodale, a young up and comer. According to the write up, she was slated for great things. The opening act was a comedy virgin. Dean Wrecker was trying his chops for the first time on a professional stage. He was taking the spot held by Dave Feener just before he died.

Lissa looked around. "I never realized that comedy was such a big business in Edmonton. This place is packed."

The waitress came over and took their drink orders and placed a bowl of tortilla chips and salsa on the table. She looked at Lissa. "You look like a Manhattan kind of girl to me."

Lissa shook her head. "Make that a soda with Lime."

"You're kidding right?"

"Nope, sorry not drinking."

"Please tell me he's drinking," said the waitress as she nodded at Mike.

Mike looked at her and shook his head. "No, but if you bring me some milk and cookies, there's a big tip in it for you."

"Will coffee do?"

"Coffee is fine, double-double."

The waitress walked away, while shaking her head, muttering at how pathetic the couple at table ten was.

She approached the bar. "A coffee, double-double and a soda with lime for the grannies in the corner."

"Come on Tara don't be a bitch," replied the bartender, ",no one said the three drink minimum had to be alcoholic." The bartender poured the soda while Tara got Mike's coffee ready.

"Well there had better be a decent tip for this," Complained Tara, "I don't walk around in stilettos and a mini-skirt to serve coffee all night."

"No one asked you to. Now you can ram the attitude and take the orders over to the customers or I can always tell Petra that you're not being your courteous best."

Tara stuck her tongue out at the barkeep and took the drinks to Lissa and Mike.

Mike thanked her and she turned to him and growled. "Let me know if you still want that milk and cookies." Then she walked away.

Mike shook his head incredulously. "Wow, someone didn't take her Midol this morning."

"Mike! How sexist can you be!" was Lissa's retort.

"Mike nothing! She was ragging on us pretty bad about not drinking."

"Well, you did promise a large tip," Lissa warned him, "so you better deliver."

"Yea that academy performance did garner a ten spot."

***

Ron the club owner got up and introduced Dean Wrecker. Dean took the mike from Ron and started his act.

Hey all! Great night here in beautiful downtown Edmonton. The oilers are hot for the first time since Gretzky quit and went to L.A.

Whyte Street instantly becomes the Blue Mile. What are they gonna do, paint the town Red? (Collective groan from audience).

Anyway Edmonton is huge. Most of you homies might not realize how big it is here 'til you go east and visit Peterborough, Ontario. That's where I come from.

Population of 70,000. The City's not like here. (Dead silence from the audience) There's not enough people there for a serial killer to do his thing. Who is there to kill? A bunch of seniors and college students? That's a transient population if ever I saw one. Seniors go south in the winter, and come back in time for the cottagers to move in for the summer while the students are gone. You need a score card to keep track of who is who and where.

Our main employer in town is Tim Horton's. There's practically one on every corner. The only thing we have more of is nursing homes

Peterborough is where all the hicks from Apsley come to say they hit the big city.

I often wondered if at Quaker Oats if an employee goes postal, and starts to grab product off the line, and stomp on it does that make him a cereal Killer.

Dean looked out at the audience. No one was laughing. He had gotten more enjoyment at his last root canal. Was he going to die up here? Apparently they didn't appreciate the bit about the oldsters, or was it the serial killer jokes? He had no more material and felt himself going down big time. He broke out in a cold sweat and felt himself hit the floor.

***

When the young comic fainted, Ron and one of the bouncers came up to the stage and carried Dean back to the dressing remove to revive him. Ron came back and said there'd be a 15 minute intermission.

Mike sat back and groaned. "That guy sucked!" He jeered. He waved his hand and Tara approached. "I'll take my milk and cookies now," he told her, "that act gave me heartburn."

Tara nodded and said she'd get a glass from the bar and some Oreos from her locker.

She came back and delivered the goods and Mike handed her a ten dollar bill.

Lissa smiled at Mike. "Good sport," was all she had to say.

***

Back in the dressing room Ron was chatting with the freshly revived comic.

"What did you do that for?" Dean had just been given smelling salts, and was trying to erase the smell. "Shit that stuff is awful!"

"We keep it here for just occasions such as this," explained Ron, "you're not the first person to pass out onstage."

"Freakin humiliating," Dean groaned, "Was it really that bad?"

"Yes Dean it sucked," said Ron bluntly. "Most people laugh when they can relate to using a place name they know. Odds are few people here don't even know Peterborough and the surrounding area. And the serial killer bit has to go as we are in the middle of a killing spree and those jokes aren't too popular right now."

Dean groaned again at this. "I'm such a jerk! I'm really sorry I didn't know. What chances do I have of making it?"

"In the biz?" Ron asked him. "Right now I would have to say your chances aren't good without a major overhaul of your act. I can help you if you want - but no serial killer jokes. Next time I hear one outta ya, your ass hits the side-walk, capiche?"

"Righto Ron," said Dean with an emphatic nod.

"Okay Dean, I'll make you a deal, meet me across the street at Subs R Us tomorrow and we can beef up the act. You can try it out again on Saturday night."

"Great, thanks!"

Ron turned to leave, but on his way out he paused. "Tell you a secret; I fell flat on my ass the first time up there. Hecklers are easy compared to dead silence."

With that being said Ron left the room. Dean followed suit and went home.

CHAPTER 16

Suzanne had seen what had happened to poor Dean. She remembered having bad material when she first started out. Suzanne felt bad for him and had told him so. He said thanks but didn't need her pity. She had been shocked by this and emphasized that it wasn't pity but empathy. He had just shrugged and walked away. No matter, thought Suzanne, if the guy didn't want support, then she wouldn't bother.

But now it was time for her spot. Suzanne was glad she was getting the shot at the headliner, and wanted it to be good.

Hey everyone! How are you all doing tonight?

Cheers from the crowd and a drunken comment from one of the patrons about her rack.

This launched her into a speech about men and their obsessions with women's breasts.

Sure I don't have what J Lo has to offer but men often ask for a serving of bacon to go with my two fried eggs.

Chuckles from the audience.

Anyhow I come from Toronto: a place known for its smog alerts, wind chill factor, and calling in the army to clean up after a huge snowfall.

They should change their slogan for the armed forces to this.

WE ARE ARMY, HERE WE GO, FIGHT YOUR WARS AND CLEAR YOUR SNOW

I am really not sure which is worse - choking on smog or freezing my ass off. Either one will drive people under the office buildings.

Anyone here buy lotto tickets? Did you get a load of the fools dancing around like idiots when they win? My cousin won seventy thousand last year; he started doing back flips when he found out.

'Dude,' I said 'what's all this for? Ya look like a moron.'

He said 'Hell, I am rich!! I can afford to look like an idiot.'

I swear I am going to try that when I win twenty bucks on an instant win card

How many out there have pets? It's great to have a cat or a dog or a mouse or even a dust bunny. What do dust bunnies actually eat? I figured it out. Anything that ends up under your bed that shouldn't be there automatically gets to be considered dust bunny food. This includes chip bags, general garbage, wayward socks and underwear. And warn your kids, people, "Don't crawl under the bed, the dust bunnies will eat you!"

Sure it keeps them in line but you may have a pile of kids with psychiatric issues waiting for counseling in the future.

Now for those of you with real pets; did you ever notice that people are either cat people or dog people? There are two separate camps there—either cats rule —dogs drool or cats are snots, dogs are not. Absolutely an either/or situation, and the animals are at war with each other too. Cats do things to get their jollies, at the expense of the poor dog. Dogs get blamed for the stupid things cats try to pull. They always seem to be in the wrong place at the wrong time. Cats get the last laugh every time. The cartoons have the right idea. Sure Sylvester would manage to catch Tweety, but it was the cat that ended up with egg on his face.

Well that's my routine for the night. Thanks for coming out. Drive safe and see you tomorrow night.

Suzanne got off stage, and was greeted by Ron.

"So how was it?"

"Not bad, not really a bar routine but it was cute."

"What constitutes a bar routine?"

"Well, don't be afraid to talk about sex or swear a little. It won't kill ya."

"I know, but I kind of promised my folks I wouldn't perform blue or talk about sex."

Ron looked skeptical. "Well, if you insist on standing on a higher moral ground, maybe you should stick to performing for family parties. Club-goers want a release from day to day life. They come here to listen to some poor loser whine about his shitty sex life or that his boss is the biggest horse's ass. Give them even a little of that and they will love you. Hey, if you wanna bitch about me or Petra we can take it."

Ron was in the mood for telling it like it is. The stress of the killing spree was having a bad affect on business on the club. "Go home and write about what pisses you off work it into the routine," he advised Suzanne. "Try it out for size. A few shits and damns, won't kill your parents. I am just saying that if you wanna make it in this business, you have to lock your inhibitions up for an hour every night."

As much as Suzanne wanted to tell Ron he **was** being a horse's ass, she realized he was right.

"Okay Ron, you have a point," she admitted, "I guess I shouldn't just play for my folks. I want the laughs, but I only heard mild chuckling tonight. I'll go back and re-work my act. I will try out the beefed up one, the next time I work. Deal?"

"Sounds great Suz! Go get 'em tiger. You're a funny lady, I know it and so do you. Let's show the world."

With that, Ron hugged her, and Suzanne let him. Any other woman might have bitch slapped him into next week, but Suz was a good sport. She could have cried at his critique or told him to fuck off, but she took the advice like the trouper she was.

Sue grabbed her stuff and headed home to re-work the act as Ron headed toward the stage to do his bit.

CHAPTER 17

Jason Tyler was in a shitty mood. He had gone out with the guys after the restaurant closed the night before. No real hell-raising, just a few beers and no one got overly wasted.

When he crawled in at three a.m. he was blasted by an ill wind from his girlfriend. He vaguely recalled that the little woman had been in a highly hormonal state and had read him the riot act. Wanting nothing to do with her at that point, he grabbed his pillow and a blanket and headed for the living room. However, sleeping on the short, lumpy, smelly couch sucked supremely. Even the dog avoided that couch.

Today he had a horrid headache and the feeling that something was going to go wrong. Very wrong.

He was trying to convince himself the fact that he didn't feel ready to go onstage that night was all about sleep deprivation. Every molecule of his body craved sleep. Christine was merciless this morning and sent him out on errands. Jason felt clearly anxious and could not ease his mind at all. But he knew deep inside it wasn't just a severe lack of sleep.

It had started the night before. He had felt that someone was following him while he was delivering food, and also on the way home from the bar. It must be all the killings going on in Edmonton. Not just the moron attacking comics but the crime rate in general was up in the city. It really didn't pay to watch the news or read the paper these days. It just leads to panic and fear mongering. The crap in the paper was way worse than what was necessary. If it weren't for the no killer jokes rule both comedy clubs had adopted, he could have build a big routine on fear mongering.

Of course, there was no greater fear, he thought, than facing Bobby the bruiser on the playground. Having your lunch confiscated and shoved down your shorts was scary enough, especially after Bob and his cronies have just scared the shit out of you. No one wants to eat after that. He and the other nerds had tried to get a support group together. Only one problem; they were petrified of each other too. In total he logged more time in the principal's office—more for protection than discipline – than the bullies did. Maybe I should have been paying protection fees to the school board, he thought. These were all good ideas for a comedy routine, though Jason would have to put a club acceptable spin on things if he chose to use it.

As Jason entered Comic Fix he saw a strange looking dude skulking around the outside of the club. He really should ask if the man needed assistance, but there was always a chance that he might be the slasher, brave enough or ballsy enough to hide in plain sight; perhaps scoping out the talent or looking for his next victim

Besides, why take unnecessary chances these days? The last thing he wanted was a bunch of cops standing over his bloody corpse saying, "*Tsk tsk Jay, you really walked into that one.*" He stared down the dude hoping the little mope would just go away. The man stood still and stared back, before he extended his middle finger and walked away.

"Friggin' weirdo!" Jason yelled after the guy.

Just as he was saying that Shelley was walking down the street toward the club.

"What the hell was that all about?" she asked him.

"Just some kook lurking around," Replied Jason, "I just wanted him to get the hell out of here. I think we should tell Jeff about it."

Shelley looked at the guy walking away. She thought she saw something familiar about his gait; her ex, Charlie walked like that. "Yeah, could be nothing but Vince Vetters had said to report everything; no matter how trivial."

Jay jotted down some notes as to the strange guy's attire and his general appearance, just in case the police wanted details. According to his nerdy armchair detective days, they usually wanted the facts.

Just one more thing to add to the already pissy day he was having.

"So ya ready for the big show in a week?" Shelley asked Jason.

Jason grimaced. "I wish I could say 'gonna kill them' or 'out for blood' but death humor is out of the question."

"Not completely," Shelley pointed out, "I think general references to death are sort of okay; just no jokes about the recent murders."

***

Jason got up onstage for a sound check and ran through his bit. Shelley found herself laughing at his routine on bullying. It was a serious subject, but then again so was insanity.

"*Hey another great night at Comic F/X. Welcome all. By show of hands any one ever been bullied?*" *Jason looks out and sees one person sitting there with no hand raised,* "*So sir does that make you a bully or an extortionist?*"

The audience gave a collective chuckle at the poor schlep's expense.

The man just sits there and says nothing, so Jay just lets it go as the gentleman doesn't appear interested in friendly banter.

"*I was a bullied child. I knew my status started going south when my teddy bear kicked me out of bed. Later in life –like at 8--I encountered Bobby the bruiser.*

Bobby showed early signs in a promising career as a Mafia henchman. If love is a battlefield then the school playground is a war zone; every nerd for himself. Even girls were potential victims. I made the mistake of trying to rescue a poor damsel in pigtails, only to have her turn around and kick my sorry ass.

"I logged a lot of time in the principals office. This was not for disciplinary purposes; it was more of a protective custody issue. I decided to be proactive with this predicament and started a support group for other victims –two problems: One, Location--Location--Location— our misguided idea that the bussing area was a great place for meetings. This was where my lunch was confiscated daily and shoved down my pants after Bobby and his minions systematically scared the shit out of me—that made me lose my appetite right there anyway. The second problem was that the bullied kids were afraid of each other.

The audience was clapping loudly. Jason was getting some laughs here.

"Talking about bullies ... the biggest bullies have got to be the big ones. Forget Dracula or Frankenstein—I'm talking about Rubber face, Freddy Krueger and Michael Meyers—and the dude with the hockey mask. One movie with these guys is more than enough, but they had to make sequels. Personally I don't see the entertainment value in spending my hard earned welfare dollars on getting the crap scared out of me. My folks put a moratorium on seeing horror movies, even at home—they said that watching them caused me and my brothers to sleep with the lights on. This drove the electricity bill through the roof.

I did find some of the cheesier slasher movies to be entertaining. I remember one where a guy was chowing down on his victims' throat –He looks up from his handy work, the first thing on his mind— 'WOW I COULD HAVE HAD A V8!!!'

Thanks everyone you were great!"

Jason left the stage to a standing ovation.

They liked him. They really liked him. The standing ovation really sealed the deal that he might just make it in stand up. This instilled a lot of confidence that he was more than just a freaking class clown. Stick that where the sun don't shine Mr. Tavares.

Tavares had been the idiot teacher sending his sorry hide down to Mr. Johnson the VP at his high school. Vice Principal was the official title, but every one said it stood for Virgin Prick –all dressed up and never been laid. Good one—he'd have to write that down and use it in an act some time.

Shelley met him at a table and clapped him on the back.

"Fantastic stuff Jay!"

"Really?" Jason was ecstatic at this news.

"You better believe it! Two things most people can relate to—bullying and horror flicks. Nice segue way from topic to the other. You should use it for the benefit –it'll get a lot of laughs."

"Okay, I was looking for something powerful for that," said Jay enthusiastically, "this is good. Well, I have to jet. I'd stay and watch your act but Christine is very pregnant and very hormonal. I came home late last night and she chewed my ass off. I am running out of body parts."

Jason reminded Shelley to tell Vetters and Jeff about the strange man they had seen outside the club and handed her his notes for a description.

Shelley wished him luck and sent him home.

***

Outside, the killer was waiting for his prey.

He had been in the club watching what he thought had been dismal display of comedy. Bully my ass! He had decided that this was the young man's comic swan song. No one calls me a bully and gets away with it! He thought. And so far as the bit about movie slashers – he would show the asshole how the job should be done. Tonight was Jason's night.

The killer had his hand on the knife hilt. He had changed his weapon of choice; now it was a dagger. Even killers can get online and research these things. Having said that, a boning knife would have the effect he wanted - dead is dead after all. The weapon might have changed but there would be no doubt to the police that a serial killer was at work.

He had considered heckling the young comic during his act, but he didn't really want any undue attention just yet. The way things were going in town he had heard that the cops were attending performances at each of the two clubs. Ha! And there he was right under their noses.

Bunch of pansies! *A lot of good your surveillance is doing, assholes!*

Besides all this, there the obvious reason why he wanted Jason dead: Jason and the lady comic had seen him outside the club. While he couldn't be certain, he thought he saw them conversing about him, and pointing in his direction and making notes. So in that case, dispensing of possible witnesses was tantamount. If he still had the notes on his person, Jason was going to get frisked. If not he would step up his plans for the lady comic and the boyfriend.

All in good time; anticipation of a righteous kill was part of the fun. Florrie didn't raise an idiot.

He was a sicko but not an idiot.

CHAPTER 13

Jason stepped out of the club. He started walking briskly as it was a bit cool and he wanted to get home to Christine. Not that he was afraid of getting his ass chewed off again, but he just wanted to be home with his girl.

Jason knew that Christine understood that his jobs kept him out late no matter which one he was doing at the time. But he also realized the closer she got to the due date, the more antsy she was about being alone. After last night's reaming he decided his main priority would be her, and not getting out with the guys. He would devote time to them as a couple before the baby came along. As much as he needed the 'me time', Chris needed him and he would deliver on that.

As Jason walked along, he thought he heard footsteps behind him, and his mind was forced into the present. While his mood had improved since his set he was still a little freaked by the guy outside the club. He was getting paranoid, he told himself. There were enough people on the street that he shouldn't be worried. All he had to do was get to the parking garage down the street. Ironically it was the same garage that Phil was murdered in. What are the chances that would happen twice with in a month? Just the same, Jason picked up his pace and kept going. Just a few more feet and he'd be at the car. He lit a cigarette took a few puffs –God these native ciggies were shitty—cheap, yes but tasted and smelled like shit mixed with sweet grass. He tossed the half smoked cancer stick and kept going. Finally he reached the car park. The old Ford was parked a few feet away.

He stepped out to insert the key in the door and felt the tip of the blade at his back.

Shit this is the last thing I need tonight –I could go down fighting unlike his other victims. I am either getting mugged or it's the reaper coming to get me.

"Turn around," was what he heard.

"Just take my wallet asshole—"

"Don't want the wallet wise guy."

Jason turned around hoping to surprise his assailant—if he was going to die he was going to make this little turd work for it. The baby would know his father loved him enough to try and take the killer down "–It's you! You were in the bar!"

"Yeah and I have to tell ya –your routine sucked!"

"Bullshit, it did!"

"You stood there and mocked me, as I watched you massacre the art of comedy. I am only gonna tell you this, as I am going to kill you anyway. The same thing I tell all my victims. YOU ARE NOT FUNNY."

With that the killer plunged his knife into Jason, pulled it out and ran.

What he didn't do was make sure Jay was dead.

Jason slid down the driver's side of the car. He knew he had little time but managed to call 9-1-1 and give his location. He heard people coming so he uttered a loud guttural yell for help. People came running and he said weakly he had been stabbed.

Jay heard sirens blaring and his world went black.

***

Two blocks away, Lissa and Borneo were on patrol when the 9-1-1 dispatch came through.

"Shit, not again!" was Mike's response.

"We don't know that for sure," said Lissa.

"Get real Cassway," was the impatient reply, "it's a block and a half away from Comic F/X. Too much of a coincidence if you ask me. Now let's go." Mike sounded the siren.

"9-1-1 said the victim was still alive," he observed. "That's a first."

"Well let's get there before he croaks," was Lissa's retort.

When they arrived at the parking garage the ambulance had arrived. The captain had been on duty at the club with another officer. Jason was in the ambulance and the paramedics were monitoring the situation and trying to stop the flow of blood from the victim. Jason was unconscious but still alive for the time being.

The captain looked remotely pleased that the killer had screwed up this time. The two witnesses were speaking to the other detective on duty. They were informed that Jason has said Shelley knew about the guy. They didn't know who Shelley was but made a note to tell the authorities.

Jason was whisked away to the hospital. The closest one was the University Hospital. It was Jason's best bet in surviving. The guy's girlfriend would have to be contacted. Cassway and Borneo were sent to the club to talk to Shelley about the info she had and to get Jason's info from her as well.

"Let's just hope this gives us the break we need to catch the squirrel," said the captain as he headed off to the hospital.

Cassway and Borneo entered the club and asked the bouncer where the owner or manager was. They were told that Mr. Beals was not in that night but Miss Morgan was in the office. The bouncer pointed to the hallway and the officers made their way to deliver the bad news about the latest victim.

Shelley was just coming out of the office when Cassway and

Borneo approached her. Seeing them in uniform meant that they were there on official business.

Nervously she asked the officers if Wally had finally crossed the line and started to serve minors.

The two young police officers looked at her quizzically.

"No, we need contact information for Jason Tyler's girlfriend Christine," Lissa told her.

Shelley immediately paled, not needing to hear anything further to get a very bad feeling about what was to come.

Lissa motioned her to the office and had her sit down. "Miss Morgan, Jason's been attacked."

"Is he...?" Shelley didn't want to finish that question. She was afraid to voice her fears.

But Lissa shook her head. "No, he's still alive - but barely. We need to get his home information and get in touch with her before it's too late."

"I am going with you. She'll need extra support." Shelley grabbed her purse and her jacket. She also wrote down Jay and Christine's address and telephone number.

"Why is that? I mean why the extra support?" was Borneo's question.

Shelley looked at them gravely. "She's very pregnant that's why."

CHAPTER 19

Jason was being treated for his life-threatening wounds in trauma Room one.

The prognosis was not looking at all good for the young comic. Once they had been furnished with information by Lissa and Borneo, the Captain and Myra Swift had gone to talk with Christine, Jason's fiancée. They had escorted her to the hospital as they were concerned that the shock would compromise her health and that of their unborn child. The doctors understood that she needed to see Jay before he died; however, they were still worried that it would be too much. At least if she went into labour early she would be in the right place. Jeff and Shelley were with her waiting to see what was going on with their friend and fellow comic.

Shelley had called Jeff at his home and asked him to meet her at the hospital.

But by the time Jeff reached the hospital, it was already too late.

After an hour and a half of trying to stop the bleeding from the brutal stabbing, the chief resident had called the time of death as 12:05 AM. Upon hearing the news, Christine had passed out and was admitted. Jay's parents were contacted about his death. They too were on their way to the hospital to say good bye to their boy and be there for Christine.

Shelley and Jeff felt for Christine; but they themselves were also devastated by Jay's death. After Phil Vetters, this had been the second comic they had worked with who had fallen victim to the maniac. Jeff was spitting mad and wanted to kick serious ass - both of the killer, and some of the officers that had been put in place. Maybe anger was too strong an emotion, however he was frustrated that one more comic had fallen prey to the killer even after the security precautions at the Club Jason had managed to tell EMS and cops that the suspect had managed to get in to the club to see his act and had even been able to jot down a description of the stranger outside the club before he lost consciousness.

At least now they had something of a description to go on, and a police artist would be used this to create a composite sketch from this description. The sketch could then be shown on the news and to the staff at both comedy clubs.

It was a start at least. Maybe they could catch the filthy animal doing this before more people had to die.

The chief called a task force meeting for the next day to discuss strategy in light of these events. The news of yet another death in the entertainment community had hit hard with the group.

The chief had let it be known that it wasn't the fault of the group. They were dealing with a smart perp. "However what the squirrel doesn't know is that the latest victim saw the guys face and managed to give a description. A police artist has been given the description and will come up with a composite sketch. From there we have the option of showing the picture to the media. Now the way I see it, this will get the community involved to call in tips but it must be stressed that they cannot approach the guy and run the risk of getting killed. This plan is good in that it brings the asshole to justice sooner thus saving lives. The downside is that our mope could be a news watcher and thus he will go underground or find a disguise and fool us even more.

"Yeah, leave us eating poop." this from the forum in the room.

"Agreed," said Vince from the back of the hall.

The chief acknowledged their points and continued. "This leads us to the second option which consists of keeping the picture to ourselves and the club owners."

"What does that do?" asked one member of the group.

"It ensures that he won't go to ground if he sees his shadow," this was the dry comment from another member.

"Seems the room is full of comedians today," replied the captain.

Vince spoke up. "If I may interject, I'd like to play devil's advocate for a minute. There is a chance that our squirrel might be a publicity hound. He might want to see his ugly mug on TV. If we deprive him of knowing that we acknowledge his part in this drama, he might go on killing just to see his name in lights —seek his fifteen minutes of fame.

I want to see as many lives spared, and spare the anguish of as many family members as possible. Every time my family hears of another death it makes my sister-in-law Peg and my parents relive losing Phil all over again. I want this mug's picture out there and let the public see what they are up against. For the sake of the city please just catch the mutt!"

The captain saw that Vince had a valid point, as did a good number of the task force.

"Okay, all in favor of releasing the composite to the media raise your mitts."

The chief noted that ninety percent voted in favor of this option. It was a clear message to him that they wanted the nightmare over with. Frankly, so did he, if the truth be known.

"Okay so it's settled," he announced, "the composite will be released to the media. It will also be posted in the staff rooms at each of the precincts in the districts in and around Edmonton proper. The staff at each of the clubs will post this in the staff rooms and the green rooms for the comics."

The captain adjourned the meeting, and the members dispersed to do their jobs.

Chapter 20

That evening Mike and Lissa were standing in line with the other patrons. They were doing another shift at one of the clubs. This time they would be visiting Comedy F/X and Vince and his partner were due to show up at The Laff Attak. It was good to have a rotating crew in case the killer was lurking and would catch on to the plan. They didn't want to run the risk that the squirrel would run to ground and leave them picking their noses.

"There's nothing worse than a police force left with rotten egg on its face," said Mike.

"Yeah and with our thumbs up our asses while some moron is running around slashing innocent people," was Lissa's response.

"I didn't become a cop just to be made to look like an ass." Mike grumbled.

"Do you need to be a cop to do that, Mikey?" Lissa ribbed him

"No, but my wife reminds me of that daily. She says merely by virtue of being a married man alone makes me an ass."

Lissa laughed out loud.

"Then I take her to bed and remind her why she married me."

"Whoa, Mikey!!" said Lissa, still laughing, "T.M.I!!"

"T.M.I? What's that?" asked a puzzled Mike.

"Too much information; It leaves me with a visual I just don't want." Lissa shook her head at the mere thought of her partner bringing on the thunder with his wife.

"Okay, 'nuf said. I'll shut up now."

"Good, thank you, at least you have a love life!!!"

They queued in silence for a while, before something occurred to Mike and he chirped up. "Ever hear of Lavalife.com?"

"Ha!" exclaimed Lissa with disdain, "Match websites? It's crap all of it! Weapons of mass self-destruction if you ask me! I have better opportunities in the produce aisle at Supersaver or my laundry room. I even get a cheap thrill or two squeezing the Charmin. Highlights of my weekend are spent with Mr. Clean."

Mike spoke up at this. "Yep, I swear the lemon fresh smell is an aphrodisiac for the Mrs., I get lucky on cleaning days."

"Must be something in the Windex; that gets me going too!" commented a woman behind them."

"Hey are we having an open mike night out here?" Suzanne was going into the club, as she heard the laughter.

Lissa had to admit the stuff they were coming up with was quite good. "Want me to write it down?"

"Sure, always looking for fresh stuff."

With that the bouncer let the crowd in.

***

The crowd inside was gearing up for a great show. Suzanne had agreed to do a spot at Comic F/X until a replacement for Jay had been found. The staff was still feeling Phil's loss and now Jay was gone as well.

Suzanne had thought about what she had heard outside the club and was going to work the singles scene bits into her act as Ron had suggested boosting the material. Someone out there would appreciate a comic spin on dating vs. picking produce in the grocery store and how Mr. Clean was her dream man —Every woman wants to come home to a bald muscled guy willing to clean floors --- after all studies had shown that a woman's fantasy involved two men-- one cooking and one cleaning. If more guys would go the extra mile maybe they might just get some.

CHAPTER 21

The hunt continued, but the police were frustrated on several fronts. The mayor was climbing down their throats about the serial killings. The old expression about shit running downhill was really ringing true. The very fact that the heat was coming down from the mayor himself meant that the Chief of Edmonton's finest was breathing down the neck of the task force put in place to catch the knife wielding maniac. The only decent lead so far had been a description of a suspicious character lurking outside Comic F/X the night Jason Tyler was killed. Ironically, this was provided by the latest casualty himself.

Unsurprisingly, morale was low at the clubs. The comics were getting up and doing their thing, but in their minds they felt like sitting ducks. They feared that the fruitcake responsible for three deaths could very well show up in the clubs and go postal. But at the same time, the comics were troupers; so they kept going.

Everyone in Edmonton was gearing up for the fund raiser in a week's time. A few moderately known Canadian humorists were slated to show up for the good cause. A big name comic was slated to play emcee for the festivities. The rumor that Jim Carrey or Mike Meyers might appear was keeping the city a-buzz with a sense of excitement.

This event was the one thing holding the comic community together.

Shelley, for one, felt like packing up her wagon and going home 'til the squirrel was caught. However, as a tribute to Phil, Dave Feener and Jason, she felt the whole "the show must go on" mantra vibrating through her soul.

Hank Cavanaugh, on the other hand was pissed to no end that the upcoming festival was getting more airtime than his recent activities. How dare they put the very people he was trying to wipe out ahead of his deadly genius on the nightly news? It would serve them right if he built a bomb and took everyone out at once instead of one knife stroke at a time. The idiots who drew the portrait had the cajones to get the picture wrong. *That is not my nose for Pete's sake! Bunch of freaking morons!*

Hank turned his attention back to the internet where he was researching pipe bombs. Maybe he should consult the Taliban on this one. After all they were proving themselves proficient at constructing improvised explosive devices. He laughed at the very thought of aping the actions of the biggest enemy of the western world since the end of the cold war.

In the end they would regret messing with good old Hank. Even Florrie would be impressed with the irony of it all.

He was still regretting not stopping to make sure his last victim was dead before he left the scene. The only saving grace in that had been that the guy later croaked in the hospital.

Well he would make sure that didn't happen again. That screw up sort of left him with his pants down, and he spent the night listening to old Florrie bitch at him for his mistake. There hadn't been enough Tylenol in the house to rid him of **that** headache.

The very thought of his pants down brought him to the "Shelley" situation. He was looking forward to demonstrating who exactly the bigger man was where Jeff Beals was concerned.

And he wanted to have his fun with her before the festival where every one was gonna croak anyhow. He might have to move on that plan sooner than later. Maybe in the next couple of days; after all he hadn't partaken of a woman in awhile.

Meanwhile back to the bomb-making. He had just come across a design for a bomb that would take out the whole convention center if he made five or six of them.

This was goanna be huge - big enough to blow a hole in the Big Bang Theory!

CHAPTER 22

Once again one of their own had been felled by a killer's knife. Jason didn't even get the chance to show his stuff at the benefit for the others. Instead he was one of the victims and his family would reap part the funds being raised.

Jeff Beals was beyond pissed off at this point; three people had already died at the hands of a sociopathic monster. He would never be able to figure out what made these animals tick. Was it abuse as a child, or just plain bad wiring at conception? Did the parents have loose screws that some how filtered into the gene pool, or was the idiot they were dealing with just a loser of the worst sort? He wanted to think the guy was a loser, as he didn't want to feel sorry for the asshole when he went on trial. In all reality he wished somehow the police would be forced to kill Mr. Psycho and not waste the tax payers' money on a trial or prison.

Jeff got his mind on something more pleasant. The Comedy Fest was all planned and his comics were ready, as were the comics working at the Laff Attak. Several big name comics had answered the call to perform for a good cause. There had been auditions for several up and coming faces to lend their talents too. It was going to be a big one and they were giving the comedy channel and CBC permission to televise it with permission of the families. At first they were going to keep it small and private but as soon as the word got out, the event became a media circus gone haywire. Jeff wouldn't normally advocate for families' sorrow to be played out on national TV, but Phil, Dave and Jason's families said to go ahead as way of saying a collective "Up yours!" to the killer.

***

Borneo and Lissa were becoming comedy junkies as a result of their assignment with the task force. Borneo said that it beat the hell out of routine patrols every night. He even thought of doing an open mike night somewhere. Maybe doing a routine about the loneliness of a patrol officer and the biggest thrill of the night being the choice of donuts at Tim Horton's, or maybe the crappy excuses people gave him for speeding or driving under the influence.

Lissa's response was not to quit his day job just yet. "Everyone thinks they have a shot at the big time at some point in their lives Mike", she told him, "You're not alone."

"But it would sure beat driving around the city waiting for some jerk to screw up, just so we can have some fun," complained Mike, "Cabbies have more fun than we do some nights. Maybe I should be a cab driver."

"Nah cabbies get robbed and killed." Lissa replied, "On the other hand, who the hell would climb into a patrol car voluntarily? And we have no money so they can't rob us."

"Well if anyone ever did try, I'd drive him right to the psych ward. That would be exciting." Mike answered. "Most of the time the wife asks me what happened on the shift, and nine times out of ten my answer is absolute squat! She stopped asking after awhile. If it weren't for the serial Killer my job would be dead."

Lissa yawned. "At least you have someone to tell. I have the cat and my houseplants to share this news with, and if they start answering back, I am driving myself to the hospital."

With that the radio went off for a call to an accident. Maybe tonight things would heat up. The only thing they didn't want to hear was that another murder had been committed.

CHAPTER 23

The cops weren't going to get their wish. Hank was sitting in the back of the Laff Attak wearing a disguise. Since Jason, the now deceased asshole, had given a description to the police before he croaked, Hank was forced to sport a three day growth of beard, a non-descript trucker's cap and clothes he wouldn't otherwise be caught dead in.

Caught dead! Ha! Good one! How ironic is that, since I'm responsible for three fatalities already? And there's more to come! Maybe if I really want to be recognized for my work I should adopt a nickname. 'The Grim Reaper'; that's got possibilities. If I left my name on the playbill next to the body the cops would know exactly who they were messing with.

Meanwhile the pipe bombs he made were ready to go. He had had a hard time getting the fertilizer at this time of year. Hank had gone to every large garden centre in the city looking for the stuff. Finally someone had gone out back and found a few bags left from last season. He had explained that it was for a special greenhouse project. Thankfully the clerk seemed not to care why he needed it. The kid was just a high school student, who probably watched MTV more than the news.

Hank was itching to strike again before the big festival. *And why not give the cops a reason to go to work instead of parking their asses at the local donut holes? That shit is bad for you anyway.*

Tonight was a comic showdown at the Attak. The top three as voted by the audience were to perform at the Festival in a week's time.

The female comic on stage, Kim Vanier wasn't bad as far as comics go. She had promise to go places in the biz. He'd keep his mind open about her. Hank hadn't killed a female yet. Like Shelley, the woman who obsessed him, she was young and pretty, but he didn't really feel like offing a girl just yet.

He was saving that for Shelley.

Kim finished her set and went to grab a drink at the bar. *No, not tonight sweetie,* Hank thought to himself, *maybe another time.*

Hank turned his attention back to the stage. The older man getting up went by the name of Squid Maloney, a retired sailor. Maybe he would be a worthy victim.

Hey how's everyone? Great crowd, thanks for coming out for a great cause.

By applause, are there any ex or retired military here tonight? Did ya have a hard time adjusting to civilian life? Several men and women applauded at this request.

I did —I figure a 58 yr old ex sailor —who wants to hire me?

So now I get to channel surf all day.

I have to admit I am damn good at it. I can get from ESPN to TSN sports net in 5.6 seconds

My routine starts at 6 a.m., even now. I get up with the little woman, have breakfast and pat her behind on her way out to work – and then I hit the couch for a marathon of game shows. Right after I discard the latest incarnation of her HONEY DO list....

The men in the audience groaned at the mention of a "Honey do" List, then they laughed at the idea of the comic being victim of the same fate.

One day I had a nightmare after discovering the sports channels were jammed, and I was forced to watch Young and the Restless. I can't decide whether Victor Newman is the Devil incarnate or the figment of my imagination after sampling too many international beers. I have decided though that there should be a new mental illness category—Post Traumatic Reality Disorder –this usually is triggered by an entire afternoon of daytime dramas and then calling my wife 'Nicky'. Not wise when her name's actually Susan

The women in the audience laughed at the reference, the men exercised boredom and a stony silence.

After that verbal misstep, my wife threatened to sell my couch so I would get off my lazy butt. She had a few offers as long as the couch potato was not included. However, some offered to pay more if the couch potato would do dishes. My wife knew a good deal when she saw one, and sent me packing.

That went well for a week, until they sent me home for greeting the lady of the house at the door wearing nothing but a tool belt.

So there, back at home. I was lying on my new couch, which fits my behind very well now, watching ESPN when the doorbell rang. Upset by being bothered I looked through the peephole in the door and saw two young ladies and decided to check them out. I opened the door and was surprised when they backed up. Forgot I just had my shorts on. Oh ya - and had that hair sticking up in the back like Spanky from the little rascals. Well, they said they wanted to introduce me to their God. And for just a small donation they would give me literature that would change my life.

I thought for a bit and told them that if they would come in I would give them an experience for free that would change their lives!! Never seen two ladies run so fast!!!!!!!

Morale of this story is - Nothing is free and don't mess with a retired sailor when he is eating chips and drinking a beer during the day!!!

The crowd loved that comic, but Hank had already decided that the retired old salt was going down.

***

As routines went Squid thought he had done quite well. He would find out later in the evening if he had a chance of going on to the benefit. It would be his way of helping with a worthy cause if he did win. And if he didn't, well he had a blast performing anyhow.

A bunch of his navy buddies had dared him to try out. Squid had been a cut up on the ship

and every one of them had said he should go into show biz when he retired. No, he had said, he was going to turn his ship mop to one at home instead.

Squid was out back having a smoke behind the club, trying to relax as Hank approached. "That stuff will kill ya, ya know?"

"Yeah I know," was Squid's retort, "but what's it to you?"

"I was just thinking that if you wanted to croak that badly there are quicker ways to pull it off."

Squid looked around nervously to see if they were alone.

Normally nothing scared him. He had faced attacks from a Russian sub during the cold war, but this was something else. He would have gladly given his life for his country, but to die like a wuss in a back alley was not in his plans. This guy was freaking him out and he stubbed out his smoke and made a run for the street. Unfortunately being fifty-eight, and packing extra beef since retirement had made getting away harder; before he realized it, the weirdo had him in a headlock with a knife at his throat. Squid thought of begging but no, if this asshole was bent on killing him, no amount of pleading was going to make a difference.

Squid heard the killer whisper in his ear. "I was going to do you a favor and kill you quickly, but running from your fate means that I am going to let you die a slow, painful death."

With that he slit Squid's throat and left him to bleed out.

Beside the body lay a playbill for that night's show. It was signed by the Grim Reaper.

Karen Vaughan

CHAPTER 24

Four murders and no leads were making the chief of police an unhappy guy. The Mayor was breathing down his neck. The expression 'shit runs down' really applied here, as he was going to read the riot act to the members of the task force if they didn't get their collective asses in gear.

Everyone working at the comedy clubs were getting especially antsy after Squid Maloney had met his violent end.

Shelley usually feared nothing or next to it. However as people kept dying, and the killer remained at large she became more insecure. The next time she got on stage could very well be her last. Every time she did her routine she wondered if the ass-wipe doing all this was watching her. Shelley hated fear and uncertainty and feeling this way was pissing her off. To make matters worse, Jeff was away at a business owner's symposium for two days so she was on her own. Normally she would enjoy a bit of 'me' time with Bruno, however with a knife wielding maniac on the loose, she was not feeling any comfort in personal time. She was planning on going home tonight to catch some sleep. Practically living with Jeff and having endless joyful sex with him was taking its toll on her rest time. Maybe she would get some much needed sleep over the next couple of days.

Shelley was getting ready to go on for her set when she saw a familiar face in the audience. It was Gord-O, the asshole from the first show she ever did at the Comic F/X. Oh god she thought, was he going to give her a hard time? That was the last thing she needed tonight. If Gord even tried to heckle her she would certainly make sure the sorry SOB was shown the door. One signal from her would alert the bouncers to do their thing. Shelley was in no mood to take crap from anyone tonight.

Just then a frightening thought occurred to her: "What if Gord was the killer?" He certainly seemed to have a hate on for comics, and saw himself as a comic genius. Shelley knew that brains weren't this guy's selling feature (along with a severe lack of sex appeal), so she really didn't think Gord could mastermind a sneeze let alone a killing spree. However, maybe she should voice her concerns to Jeff, who would forward it to Vince Vetters. As she couldn't afford this thought to wreck her night, Shelley got on stage prepared to give her best.

Hey all, how's downtown Edmonton tonight? Applause and cheers from the crowd *Great!*

Things are going well in my life.

I'm currently in a relationship. It's about time. I enjoy my own company, but after a while even I can handle only so much time with myself. After a while even the batteries get bored with me.

When you're dating someone, you're always waiting for the moment the other person is going to say they've had enough. Men never say the words 'We have to talk.' I had a boyfriend where the only conversations we had involved monosyllabic grunts while pleasuring each other, polite dinner conversation, and fighting. Other than that, he really didn't have much to say. It made me feel like I was dealing with Captain Caveman. So when the time came to issue the inevitable "It's not you it's me" I was shocked that he could string a sentence together. So there it was, those magic words. It's not you it's me.

My reply: "*Damn straight it was you! It was always you.*" Men always believe the women think they're wrong. I was just being agreeable.

What about the response to "I just want to be friends"? That could be: *I am so glad you hold me in such high esteem, because I really can't stand you!*

Then there are boyfriends who have the gall to hold a grudge for telling him to bugger off. I had one who claimed he didn't hold grudges---That's because he had them tattooed on his arm so he could recall them at will.

Since I showed the ex the door I haven't dated anyone. I have seen so many female friends go through multiple partners. What happens when you're sleeping with five different guys—do ya write the names on your arms just to keep them straight? I see a problem here—

I don't have the best of memories for names. Now most of the time I can get away with darling, sweetheart, "Oh God's gift to women", but there are certain times – like when you say goodbye the next morning – when it is socially expected that you will use the other person's name.

I finally found a solution to this. I just wrote the guy's name somewhere on my person and could easily refer to it for those times of mandatory usage. This was working fairly well for me until one week when I was blessed with a rather active social life. Well thanks for an amazing time (check right shoulder) Steve. [Notice puzzled look. Quickly check left shoulder.] Brad. [I went through arms, midriff, thighs...] Let's just say that I ended up taking off so much clothing that we ended up back in the bedroom again where "Oh, God!" seemed to be the moniker most used. Actually, I realized later that the name I was trying to remember was David. - Although if you ask me he should have been called Goliath!

Shelley waited for the other comics to do their thing and got up for the last set of the night. She was relieved that Gord-O hadn't said a word during the break-up bit. She even noticed that he had gotten up through her second act and left, much to her relief.

Shelley left through the back door close to where her car was parked. She had just shut the door behind her when an arm came around her neck and tightened.

"Let go!" Shelley said, trying to remain calm. She knew instinctively who was behind this attack. "Gord, I know it's you, so just F-off and go and I won't say a thing. You need serious help."

Gord didn't tighten his grip on her but neither did he do as Shelley asked. What was she expecting? A guy who would actually listen? Who was she kidding? So instead of trying to reason with the asshole, she tried physical force on the dude.

"Shut up bitch!" Gord was breathing hard in her ear; his breath was stale and his voice gravelly, like a 3 pack a day smoker. "Be a good girl and Uncle Gordy might show you a hell of a good time before I snap your neck. So just be quiet, or die before you experience the best sex you'll ever get."

Shelley didn't know whether she wanted to laugh or puke at the thought of Gord trying to get frisky with her. If he did try she'd give a good kick in the jewels. Gord seemed to hesitate for a minute, just enough time for Shelley to elbow him in the side and yell for help.

A man came rushing into the alleyway in order to assist Shelley. Gord was trying to catch his breath after the jab she had administered. Normally she'd never kick a man while he was down but what the hell –Shelley gave him a good hoof to the midsection, which sent him gasping and sprawling to the ground. She signaled to the stranger to call 9-1-1. Maybe they finally had the maniac.

After the guy had called for help, she thanked him for being there when she needed him.

"That's alright, honey, glad I could help. Who's the jackass?"

"Just some guy with more moxie than actual balls. What's your name, pal?"she said as she reached out to shake his hand.

"Marcus Dunn," the stranger replied, "I am on vacation; I was just leaving the comedy club around the corner. Great stuff! You Canadians have lots of things to laugh at up here."

Shelley smiled at this. "I am actually one of the comics, glad you enjoyed it."

Before Marcus could heap more praise on her performance, the police showed up.

Lissa and Borneo jumped out of the squad car.

"What do we have here?" this from Lissa.

It was Marcus who answered. "I came across this lovely young lady being brutalized by this idiot. He was trying to kill her but didn't have the guts –especially after she elbowed him."

"You okay?" Lissa asked Shelley.

"Not sure maybe I should get checked out," Shelley replied

"Want an ambulance? There's one on the way." The officer inquired.

The comic shook her head. "No that's okay, I can drive myself; my car is just over there. Besides I'm a starving artist, I can't afford the ambulance fees. Anyway you'll need it for the incredible hulk here."

But the police had no intentions of treating their new charge so tenderly, and Borneo stepped in to grab Gord and stuff him in the squad car. As this took place, Gord screamed of police brutality and threatened Shelley with charges of assault.

Borneo was in no mood to let Gord dictate events. "Shut up Mister or we'll tell all your cell buddies that a mere girl took you out with her elbow. Then they'll see what a pussy you really are."

CHAPTER 25

After the police had hauled Gord off to the precinct, Shelley had agreed to go to the hospital, but in her own car. She arrived at the Emergency ward with her savior in tow. Normally she would not allow a complete stranger in her car with her; however, the dude did save her life.

The doctors got to Shelley right away as it was not busy. The main attending physician told her she would have some bruising as Gord had tried to choke her, and asked if she wanted to press charges against him.

"Damn skippy I do," said Shelley firmly. "The asshole scared the crap out of me, and if I have damages to my vocal cords I am going to kick his ass around the block."

The doctor asked her if she wanted to get the cops in to get a statement.

"No, I'll go down to 74 Division in the morning, make a statement, and press charges. The little perverts gonna fry."

It wasn't the mere fact that he had attacked her, and the possibility that Gord-O was the killer that really pissed Shelley off. Shelley also felt violated and just wanted to go soak off the stench of her attacker and relax before trying to sleep. She had to and wanted to call Jeff. She didn't want to wait til he got home to hear it from official sources. Part of her hoped he'd get on a plane and come home just to hold her and make her feel better. On the other hand she really didn't want to seem needy to Jeff or anyone else for that matter.

Marcus was waiting for her as she came out of the ER just to make sure Shelley was okay and asked if she wanted a ride home.

"No," she said, but thanked him for helping her.

"No worries," said Marcus with a nod. "Right place, right time and all that! Glad I was there, it could have been worse."

Much worse was Shelley's thought.

"Let me do something for you in a way of saying thanks."

Marcus replied that it wasn't necessary, but Shelley insisted as it would make her feel better. They finally agreed that a complimentary ticket to a comedy show whenever he wanted at Comic F/X was an acceptable repayment.

Just then, Officer Lissa Cassway walked in.

"Hi, Miss Morgan, I have come to make sure you are okay and to see what your plans are as far as pressing charges."

"I told the doctor that I fully intend to but I want to wait til tomorrow when I am feeling refreshed, if that's okay."

Lissa confirmed that it was, and also stated that if Shelley wanted her to follow her home she would be there.

Shelley, although she knew that the perp was behind bars at least for the night, took Lissa up on the offer. Lissa commented that Borneo was waiting in the squad car and would escort her to the door.

"Why the special treatment?" asked Lissa when she was told of Borneo's escort, "it's not like I'm royalty or anything."

"Detective Vetters sort of insisted," replied Lissa. "Trust me not all crime victims get this treatment. Phil was his brother as you know and the comics were Phil's extended family therefore; when the detective found you were attacked, he sent us over. Vince and Jeff are also friends, and Jeff would have his ass if anything further happened to you. He might be a cop but Jeff scares the crap out of him."

"Yes, that's right my boss is a bully."

"Boss? Vince said Jeff was your boyfriend."

"Vince has a big mouth," Shelley replied as she signed the discharge papers. The two women headed out to the parking lot.

CHAPTER 26

Shelley went straight home from the hospital, walked into her bathroom, shed her clothes and immediately trashed them. Then she jumped into the shower and scrubbed til she was red. The ordeal could have been worse but still it had taken its toll on her emotions, and there in the shower, Shelley broke down under the hot spray and cried until there were no more tears left. Finally, She dried off and jumped into bed in her largest t-shirt (the non-company kind of pajamas).

After being violated as she had been, Shelley wouldn't have thought she'd be able to sleep, but thankfully she drifted away.

Jeff let himself in after taking the red eye home from the conference. Vince had called his cell telling him Shelley needed him. He had tried to call her home phone and her cell but got no response. By the time he got out of the taxi, he was frantic with worry.

"Shelley!" Jeff was yelling as he went through the house; he finally found her in her room curled up with the dog. both of them sleeping soundly. He didn't want to disturb them so he just disrobed and got in bed.

Feeling a presence in the room, Shelley bolted up in bed and was just about to scream when she realized it was Jeff.

"Crap Jeff, ya nearly scared me half to death!" exclaimed Shelly.

"Sorry Honey, didn't mean to," was the contrite reply, "I called out but you didn't answer."

"It was a rough night….I was attacked outside the club."

"I know about all that; that's why I came home early."

"How?" said Shelley irritably. "Which one of the damn cops has a big mouth?"

"Vince called and told me," Jeff told her, "I nearly hijacked the first plane out of Winnipeg to get here. I am afraid we won't be able to fly West Jet anytime soon."

"Well I am glad you made it. I was tempted to call you myself, but I wanted handle this like a big girl. Lissa took care of me and followed me home. I have a hero, some tourist who happened to be at the club came by as Gord was about choke me."

"Gord? That son of a bitch! I am going to kill his ass!" Jeff was furious at the thought of the moose having his hands any where near his woman. "He didn't ….ah do anything else did he? If he did, I swear I'll have his balls in a mason jar."

"Well he might have if Marcus hadn't come along when he did. I'm telling you Jeff, I usually don't scare easily but this time I could sense I was going to die."

"Well I guess I have the guy to thank for your life."

"You'll get the chance I comp'd him a ticket for tonight's show. He's going home Saturday so we only have now to repay him."

"Good," said Jeff with a firm nod, "the man is a freakin' hero for that!"

Shelley reached for him and pulled him close. If she had her way, he would help her forget the attack. Just as they were getting into it, the phone rang. Jeff told her to ignore it, but she grabbed it.

Jeff rolled onto his back cursing Alexander Graham Bell for the intrusive instrument. Shelley was off the phone soon after.

"Who in heavens name was that?" Jeff was still perturbed.

"Officer Cassway was checking to see if I was okay, and to remind me I have to go make a statement and press charges against Gord."

"Well they can wait, we're in the middle of something, and oh I was just about to fill your head with more pleasant thoughts. Let Gord hang a little longer."

With that he rolled over her and loved the bad memory away.

Afterwards Shelley showered and dressed while Jeff tended to Bruno and made some calls to the club manager to get a replacement for Shelley. She might insist on performing anyway but he wanted her to have a night to rest her throat. After all, that's what caring boyfriends do.

Jeff told Shelley she had the night off. Normally she would have argued but the docs at the hospital given her the same advice so she gave in. Let Jeff think it was his doing.

Soon after, they left to go seal Gords fate.

CHAPTER 27

The police captain and Detective Swift decided to question Gord about all the nights that the Killer had struck. They had no proof that he was responsible for the other deaths in town but it didn't hurt to check things out. They were in agreement that they didn't think he had enough smarts to pull off that many murders; however, he had attacked Shelley Morgan outside the club, and he had harassed her at work before according to Jeff Beals, the club owner at Comic F/X.

Myra started in on him, fully intending on being the bad cop. Finally, after years of letting Vince have all the fun, she got to be the mean one. The Captain was letting her too. He was quite willing to come in and clean up if things got ugly.

Myra folded her arms and glared. "Okay Gord, time to start singing."

Gord was sat in a chair chained to the table so he wouldn't go nuts on them. "What about?" He asked. He really was as dumb as he looked.

Myra was already impatient with him. "Come on, you moron! We have you for the attack outside Comic F/X last night."

"Oh that," said Gord dismissively. "The mouthy bitch

deserved it. Her and her male bashing routine; I wanted to show her that kind of stuff is not right. Kinda damages guys self esteem."

"Ooh big words for such a piss ant," Myra sneered.

"See even you're doing it. Are all you bitches alike?"

"Watch the potty mouth mister!"

"Ha, you're callin' me names, so it's only fair."

"Okay I'll play nice in the sandbox if you will." Myra was willing to back off a little and then go for the kill. Vince had taught her well. "So Gord, tell me, why last night? Why did you wait 'til last night to teach her a lesson as you say? Why didn't you whack her the first night when you heckled her? From what I heard, Miss Morgan gave back as good as she got. Made ya look like the pathetic little ....creature that you are." Myra wanted to use the term worm but thought better of it for now.

"The comedian is not supposed to heckle back;" said Gord obstinately, "it infringes on my rights to free speech."

"Since when is heckling free speech?" asked a skeptical Myra.

"It's not heckling; it's instantaneous feedback to a crappy act."

"Sure if that's what you call it." Myra thought this was turning in to a pissing contest and was ready to put it to an end.

Gord continued to argue. "It's my right as a consumer to comment on a service provided if I don't like it."

Myra banged her fist on the table as the captain walked in. Capt O'Malley just sat and watched Myra have her fun with the perp.

"Enough you worm - playing nice isn't getting us anywhere here. Is it just Miss Morgan's comedy that brings out your inner critic or do you expand your talents to other comedians?"

"No," said Gord stubbornly, "Shelley's the only one who really pisses me off."

"Come on, get real Gord! I don't believe for a minute that a guy with so much venom would reserve it to a few words—why not say slash someone's act for good if you don't like it."

Gord sat up straight in his chair. "What are you talking about? I wasn't going to kill Miss Morgan! I just wanted to teach her a lesson about male bashing that's all! I don't know anything about killing comics!"

"That's B.S. and we both know it." Myra was in full bad cop mode now and was going for his throat figuratively speaking, when the captain told her to go for coffee.

"But Sir I was just getting to the point!" Myra was incredulous. (All part of the routine)

"Yes, I saw the claws come out detective, now go!"

Myra was uttering an expletive as she opened the door.

Gord started to giggle.

"What's your problem?"

"Your boss just heckled you!"

Myra looked daggers at him and slammed the door after her.

CHAPTER 23

Gord was safely ensconced in a jail cell awaiting arraignment procedures. As promised Shelley came down to the precinct to price assault charges against him. She also gave a statement as to the particulars of the attack.

Neither Jeff nor Shelley really believed that Gord was responsible for the other deaths. However, at this stage the police really didn't want to discount the possibility as they had their doubts based on his statement during the interrogation.

Gord had no choice but to admit that he attacked Shelley, but as far as doing the other comics he said nothing and did the natural thing by lawyering up. The problem was that the police didn't have a weapon to go on and they couldn't get a warrant to search his place. The likelihood of him getting bail was poor as he was employed at minimum wage in a factory. Shelley therefore was not worried about him getting out to finish her off. People like Gord didn't get the 'Get Out Of Jail Free' cards either.

***

The news of Shelley's assault was all over the evening broadcasts and Hank Cavanaugh was watching closely.

Hank was steaming mad at the suspect in custody for two

reasons: The moron who attacked Shelley did what he had wanted to do, this angered Hank to no end; secondly the news report said that they were interested in the same individual for the comic killings.

NO! THAT'S MY THING! YOU CAN'T GIVE HIM CREDIT FOR MY WORK. IT'S NOT FAIR AFTER THE EFFORT I PUT INTO THIS!

Hank began pacing the floor, exclaiming to himself that he would go out and prove he was the one responsible. When and if they released the guy in custody Hank would get him for hurting Shelley. Shelley was Hank's job. This idiot would find out firsthand that you don't scoop someone else's kill.

Hank's brain was rammed against his skull as Florrie's voice told him what a useless moron he was. The only way he could get rid of the old nag was to go "do" another comedian that night. That's right; it was time for another self-righteous clown to bite the dust!

Hank went into his special tool box to retrieve his instrument of death, and headed out to The Club. Which one though? Last time he did Squid Maloney outside the Laff Attak; so tonight he would go visit the Comic F/X joint and maybe get to see Shelley. He wasn't ready to kill her yet; maybe the other chick with the huge rack would suffice. He hadn't killed a girl so far; maybe tonight he would.

CHAPTER 29

The Club was packed. Shelley took a seat close to the bar. She treated her self to a glass of wine tonight as she was not going on. She really wanted to but her throat was sore and Jeff was not letting her any where near a mike. Maybe if she just sat back and enjoyed the show it would be fine for sitting one night out. Suzanne and Mike were on tonight as well as one of the other new comedians who had auditioned at the same time Jason had. Shelley was dressed casual for a change, wearing jeans, t-shirt and a denim jacket; a silk scarf was in place to cover her bruised neck.

Jeff had told the staff what had transpired the night before but had urged them to respect Shelley's privacy by avoiding the subject of her attack. He also asked them if Gord had heckled any one that night. The waiters and bouncers all stated that surprisingly Gord had been on his best behavior, and that he had left quietly out the front of the club. Jeff had work to do in introducing the comics but told Shelley he would sit with her during each set.

It was no secret now that they were an item. Jeff was not giving her preferential treatment over the other staff so they really didn't care what was going on. In fact there had been wagers amongst them that the owner would "bag" the new chick soon after Shelley started. Several fifties had crossed palms at the outset of their relationship. One waiter even stated that he would give her a go if the opportunity arose. He was laughed at as Shelley needed a man, not a post –pubescent pug.

Soon after Shelley got herself seated, Marcus came in and joined her at the table as a guest of honor for the evening. Shelley bought her hero a Scotch and Coke, which he had stated was his favorite drink. Personally she thought scotch was swill, but who was she to judge a man's tastes in alcohol?

As they raised a glass, Jeff got up and did an intro to the new guy, Pete Sanchez.

Pete did an act about growing up Puerto Rican in a city slightly less cold than Churchill Manitoba and how his mama had knitted him testicle booties to keep his package warm in the winter months. He went on to say that with his Latin good looks he could find better ways to keep warm but he wasn't about tell mama that. After all imagine his embarrassment after disrobing in front of the woman of the moment to find his Willie warmer in place. The rest of the routine was a riot and Pete garnered a standing ovation for his set. Susanne went on after him and then Mike, the other new guy. The night ended with the audience raving about all three acts.

Little did anyone know Hank was sitting at the back of the club. He had decided earlier who his target was this evening and milled out of the club with everyone else. Hank had followed Susanne home a few times just to scope out a new kill site. He had the dagger ready to use and a copy of the playbill, signed and available to drop by the body. *This is going to throw off the bozos in blue.* He usually nailed his kills in the down town area but tonight he thought to let Suzie Q get most of the way home, and then jump her. She would never be expecting it this far away from the club. He found the bus stop for the route Susanne took back and forth to the club. There were several people waiting there so he was able to hide in plain sight. *Finally Florrie will see me for the genius I am!*

The bus arrived. Hank paid his fare and went to the back of the vehicle. Susannah was back there listening to her CD walkman. He sat across from her and watched from behind a book he was pretending to read.

She caught him staring at her; said to stop and called him a freak. That really made him mad and he was now determined that she would suffer plenty before he let her die. Susanne flipped the bird at him and moved to the front. The time came for her to get off through the front doors as he slipped out the back.

He slunk behind her a few paces; Hank had his hand on the knife in his pocket. When he was within a few paces of Susanne he got in behind her grabbed her around the neck, and pointed his weapon at her throat. He whispered in her ear not to scream or he'd cut out her tonsils.

"Nod if you understand me."

She did. Hank motioned her over to the bushes; pushed her to her knees, and knelt behind her with the knife still in place at her neck.

"Okay there are two things I want you know: one, I haven't killed a girl since I took my mothers life. Normally I don't hurt women but the old bag had it coming to her. This is new to me so bear with me. Secondly I need to kill some one tonight to prove to the police that they caught the wrong guy. You'd think I'd just let the dude fry for what I am doing, but it's this way; I worked really hard on planning these killings, so why should some asshole get the credit for it? I chose you for the very fact that I really don't like your act. In fact, you suck!

"But what really sealed your doom was the fact that you called me a freak and had the gall to give me the finger. NO ONE FLIPS HANK OFF WITH OUT DIRE CONSEQUENCES! Got that?"

Susanne nodded again to show she understood as she couldn't speak. Hank's hand still covered her mouth to keep her from yelling. But Hank wasn't as smart as he gave himself credit for. Susannah opened her mouth and bit down hard on his thumb. Hank yelled out in pain.

"You bitch!" He was too busy concentrating on his wound so Susanne was able to elbow him and get away. She got off her knees and ran for her life as she yelled for help. Unfortunately her assailant managed to recover and gain on her.

Hank jumped her from behind and wrestled her to the ground. He rolled her over onto her back.

He straddled her and grabbed her throat but forgot her hands were free, and Susanne scratched at his arms and finally went for his face. Hank gritted his teeth through the pain and managed to pin her arms down as he reached for his knife. Once again he held it to her throat.

"Fun's over sweetheart; it's time to die!" With that he plunged the knife into her gut again and again.

He was just about to slit her throat as he had with the others but he heard voices across the park.

Hank dropped the playbill, tossed his knife and ran. He had to get the hell out of there before they found the body.

CHAPTER 30

Right in the middle of a late night emergency task force meeting the call came in to the stationhouse that the 'Grim Reaper' had left another calling card next to a female body. There was a stir in the task force when the victim's gender was revealed - up until now the victims had all been male. Myra, the captain and the Borneo/Cassway team were called to the scene as well as CSU team #1. The Medical Examiner Watters was also called.

Given the scene's location, he two young patrol officers feared that it might be Susanne. The body had been found in the south end of Gallagher Park near 97th Ave NW. by some teens gathering for a party of sorts. Upon arriving at the crime scene, Lissa and Mike did crowd control, and Myra and the ME saw to the body while the captain interviewed the youths.

One strapping young buck named Johnny Jakes acted as the spokesperson for the group. "We were down by the concert bowl doing our thing, ya know, when we heard screaming' ya see. We booked it up the hill to find a guy straddling a person near the bushes. He or she was putting up a big fight. He was really working at it; whatever he was doing to the poor sap. He looked to have a weapon in his hand; when I yelled at him to stop he slashed his arm down to finish the job and took off. I wanted to chase the dude and detain him, but I wasn't sure if he still had that thing he hurt her with. So we just went to see if we could help her.

"Troy here," Johnny cocked a thumb at his friend, "knows CPR and emergency first aid so he tried real hard to stop the bleeding. But it was too late. She was gone, man- real gone. Trina's the one who called in; then we looked around for the weapon. Natalie spotted it while she was losing her supper in the bushes."

"I wasn't puking!" was Natalie's indignant response.

Johnny shook his head and stated to the officers that indeed she was. In turn Natalie stuck out her tongue and flipped him off.

Johnny was proud to let the captain know that he had made sure his friends didn't touch anything - sometimes watching Crime Scene Superheroes on Cable when grounded really paid off. The captain patted his arm and said he was right not to disturb the scene, and thanked troy for trying to save the victim.

"There was just too much blood, sir" was his answer.

The kids stayed put - though they kept a distance from the cops - and the captain asked them to describe the killer as Myra took notes. The Captain then conferred with the medical examiner and the team taking care of the victim. The head of CSU bagged the bloody dagger thrown by the bushes and the playbill by the body. The victim was Susanne Goodale, as they had feared.

The Captain was saddened by another kill, but at the same time was relieved that they had a weapon—finally a lead.

He called the stationhouse to confirm the findings at the park as a work of the Reaper and to ask for an artist to take a description from the kids. He then called the task force meeting being run by Vince and announced the same.

The conclusion was that it was now time to turn up the heat.

Chapter 31

Jeff and Shelley were lying in bed after another session of love making. They had heard that Susanne's body had been discovered in Gallagher Park. Some teens had witnessed the killer doing his thing and had scared him off. An attempt had been made to save Susanne by a couple of the kids but to no avail; she was already gone.

Shelley, still reeling from her own attack, was taking it hard. The sex had been less than stellar but that hadn't mattered to her. She just wanted to feel close to Jeff, and did a lot of crying. The loss of her friend and fellow comic had left her empty. And if the guy had struck while Gord-O had been in jail, that meant Gord wasn't the serial killer. Gord-o was still guilty of attacking her, of course - the charges would stick on that one; of this she was glad. But if this kept up, she was afraid there would be no one left alive to perform at the benefit.

Jeff was trying his best to console and distract her with sex. This generally worked but even he was feeling the pain. Susanne's mom had been inconsolable and had needed hospitalization. Suzie was the only girl in her family. She and her Mama had been close. While Mrs. Goodale didn't think pursuing a career as a comedienne was an entirely wise choice, she had supported Susanne's need to try it as a means to other bigger things. Susanne's brothers wanted to go out and wrench the life out of the pathetic bastard. So, for that matter did Jeff. The police reassured the boys that they were going to bring the man to justice and warned them not to play vigilante.

"I can't believe it!" sobbed Shelley. "The bastard took out Susanne. It's just not fair." Shelley had her theories as to why Susanne had been the latest victim. The Reaper didn't want Gord to get credit for his hard work, and also to prove he could do a girl comic as well as a man - an equal opportunity murderer.

"Well honey," Jeff said as he wiped at the tears running down his lover's face, "we should leave the theorizing to the police."

"Yeah, I know but still it makes sense. I took abnormal psychology in college; the Prof said anything could set a sociopathic a-hole to do what he or she does. Childhood trauma, an inferiority complex or any other plethora of sickening reasons; for instance, postpartum depression and religious beliefs have been the motives for a lot of murders.

"Wow! What made you want to study that?" was Jeff's next question.

"Would you believe I wanted to be a cop at one time?"

"You?" Jeff looked incredulous.

"Uh-huh, can you imagine me in uniform?" Shelley replied. She was propped up on one elbow and was playing with Jeff's curly chest hair.

"Hmm, can I picture you out of uniform instead? That's much more fun. I'd even let you frisk me and do a strip search. I'd happily comply."

All this talk about naughty police women was making them both excited as they rolled around and tried to forget that their friend was gone, which in the next hour or so, became quite easy.

CHAPTER 32

I started a joke, that started the whole world crying, but I couldn't see that the joke was on me.

Oh no.   Beegees.

Across the city, Hank was pacing his living room. He was pissed at himself. He had been seen doing the girl. That was just not right. He would have been able to take out one kid, but doing all five was too risky. Much worse was the fact that he had had to toss his knife in the bushes. If anyone got close enough it could easily be found.

Florrie's voice in his head was giving him a pisser of a headache. The old nag!

He knew he'd screwed up; he didn't need his dead momma screeching at him. Maybe after all this was over, he'd do himself in just to get rid of her. Killing himself was the best way to avoid incarceration for the rest of his life. Guys like him didn't get respect in prison. They became the prison bitches for every bully in the joint. He would never survive a stint in Alberta's finest penitentiary. Rape and possible murder would be his fate. He would take himself out before those asses got him. Maybe going out like a Taliban suicide bomber would be the best way. No more Florrie nagging at him and the cops could kiss his ass.

Meanwhile he would have to watch the news and see what they had on him. He had been wearing gloves so prints weren't a problem. However, the cops had the playbill and he was sure one of those kids had blabbed by now. A description of him was already out there, but he had solved the problem once by growing his beard and dying his hair ash blond. Maybe he'd just go down to Gallagher park and casually ask around see if any of the hooligans hanging around knew about the incident. Maybe they did, and then he would have to take them out. Nah, too risky - and he had much bigger fish to fry. The little brats hadn't really been close enough to see him. By the time they had yelled at him he had gotten a head start. He had hidden behind the outhouse at the park long enough to see the little farts try and save the dead girl. Soon after he heard the sirens, and he disappeared into the woods, shed his over coat and later burned it along with his hat. It was a cold night and he had managed to find an oversized Jersey in the donation bin of a nearby plaza. Hank was smart enough not to grab a bus home 'til he was way out of the area near the park.

When he had gotten home he had taken a hot shower to get rid of any traces of Susanne's blood on him. It was a shame he had to kill her - she was nearly as cute and funny as Shelley - but he'd had a point to make. . She had drawn the short straw and so she had to die. It was just a pity it had gone so badly.

Perhaps he was just feeling desperate and his hits were becoming more random. Hank saw himself as more organized than that. Good planning was key where murder was concerned., and Florrie, despite the huge nag that she had been, had always instilled good habits and the thought that if you have a job to do, you do it well. Hank's job was ridding society of people who thought they were funny but really weren't. He'd love to take out those who thought these people had a chance at a career in comedy. Alas, too many fools and so little time.

That's what bombs were for.

Maybe he'd take a break from the stabbings for now and prepare for the 'big bang' and his own swan song. He also had to deal with Shelley and the club owner before the grand finale to his show. He went to bed dreaming of this.

CHAPTER 33

Finally things where heating up in the investigation. The witnesses in the park gave a description of the person they had seen killing Susanne. This closely matched the description of the man Jason had seen outside the club the day he was murdered. The knife used in Susanne's death was the same knife used to kill Jason and Squid Maloney, yet different from Dave Feener and Phil Vetters. But the M.O.'s were too close to think that there were two killers out there. Besides, a playbill had been found at each scene so that ruled this theory out. Apart from the murder weapon, the only thing that had changed was the fact that the squirrel had given himself a title and had begun to autograph the playbills. The possibility of bringing in a profiler from the RCMP was being tossed around. The chief was looking into the budget before okaying this move.

Meanwhile the psychiatrist used during police investigations was speaking to the task force on the subject.

"Clearly our 'unsub.' (stands for 'unknown subject' which is FBI speak for unknown perpetrator) has narcissistic tendencies and wants recognition for his hard work.

The reasoning behind the change in weapons could be that

he wanted something easy to conceal and bring out just before he kills his vics. According to the M.E. on this case, the first two victims had been killed with a butcher knife based on the stab wounds. Given the description of the wounds, I'd say the guy had to work harder for the first two kills than for the subsequent murders."

"Kind of a cut and run deal, wouldn't you say doc?"

Titters arose from the audience.

"Yeah and what kind of name is the Grim Reaper? This moron is really full of himself!" an officer in the back of the room was quick to add.

"I really don't think we can afford to think of our perp as a moron," the psychiatrist continued, "clearly, coming up with a name for himself and re-thinking his choice of weapons is not the work of an idiot; hedonistic, or egotistical, possibly; stupid, no."

The task force went on to discuss beefed up safety measures to be taken at the clubs and for the benefit. Each bouncer at both clubs was to be given a composite sketch of the unsub with instructions to alert the undercover officers on site of anyone matching the description. In addition, extra security was to be employed during the Benefit.

The mood of the task force was much better this time as they thought they might be getting somewhere. While there had been no prints on the knife found at the last scene, at least they had a weapon. There had also been a tip phoned in by the bus driver who dropped Susanne at the stop just outside Gallagher Park at ten p.m. He had also said that a man had gotten off at the same time but couldn't really give a good description, except that he was medium height, stocky and was wearing a black trench coat. The bus driver didn't see his face as the individual was wearing a hat or a hood. This pretty much matched the description given by the one kid in the park. Score one for the good guys. Pleas were put out for more help or descriptions of anyone seen wearing a similar outfit on route 4 that same night or since. If indeed the perp was smarter than the average bear, he would have dumped the clothes he had been wearing for Susanne's murder. A search of dumpsters and donation bins around the area was being conducted by routine patrols.

***

Right after the meeting, Borneo and Cassway were heading for their squad car and speculating about what the likelihood of finding said outfit would be.

"Slim to none, if you ask me," was Lissa's assessment.

"Oh Swami Cassway do tell! What made you come to that startling conclusion?" Mike was full of sarcasm.

Lissa looked at him incredulously. "Come on Mike, think about it. What would you do if you were this guy? To be a good cop, sometimes you need to think like a criminal."

"Well since you asked so nicely. I would burn said clothing, or if I were the really intrepid sort. I would soak the outfit used during the crime in a bucket of lye thus taking out all stains and disintegrating the clothing. Ta da! No evidence."

"Bravo Mike! You too could pass the sergeant's exam." Lissa applauded him. "By the way, I got it!"

Mike's mouth dropped open. "Holy shit! You're a sergeant now? What am I going to do; break in a newbie?"

"Newbie? Oh you mean rookie. Yeah, I guess, eventually, when I go for my D1 badge. For now you're stuck with little old me.

Mike rolled his eyes. "What's worse, driving around with 'the Ego has landed' or teaching some one to put up with my baser habits? Good rookies are hard to come by. They're fresh out of college or the academy and think they know everything. I need some one I can mold into a good cop, and one who can fetch my coffee and donuts."

Mike realized he hadn't properly congratulated Lissa on her accomplishment and did so. He couldn't hug her while on duty but promised to throw her a party after work some night after work and invite the squad.

It was Lissa's turn to raise her eyebrows. "Fetch coffee and donuts? I never did that for you."

"My point exactly, obviously I didn't do my job!"

"Yeah right Borneo, dream on. I might add that the only thing you know about molding is the smell of your socks after an eight hour shift."

Mike made a stabbing motion. "Cuts deep Lissa, really deep; you should really revisit the comedy thing."

"Comic? No way, that shit can get ya killed around here."

CHAPTER 34

Shelley was starting to feel the stress of all the recent events. Susanne's death had really hit her hard. Up until then all the victims had been guys. The very fact that a female comic had been taken down in the city meant that she wasn't safe. This guy was turning into an equal opportunity shithead. Also, in light of her own recent attack at the hands of Gord, she was getting really antsy. Shelley would swear on her life that she wouldn't let the killer get to her; yet it was happening.

Shelley had loved her solitude at one point. The time spent relaxing at home after a hard shift at work, before becoming a comic; or the chance to review her routines since starting at Comic F/X was a balm to her. But lately she felt more secure when Jeff was with her. She hated the idea of becoming a sniveling weakling who needed a guy around to feel safe.

She had grown up in a rough part of town and was able to cope with bullies. Shelley had also taken self defense and martial arts. Nothing had really scared her in the past. Since Gord had attacked her, however, she wanted to start working out again to be prepared for a possible attack. Jeff assured her that he was there for her 24/7 if she needed him. That was what bothered her.

She wanted to have him around out of love, not just to provide her with a sense of security. Her mom, as a single parent, had always impressed upon her that a man was a nice addition to a woman's life, but not a necessity. She had taught Shelley to take care of herself, so a man wouldn't have to. Mom had also instilled in her brothers that strutting around like an alpha male was not flattering. Women do like strong men just not domineering Tarzan types.

Shelley appreciated Jeff's presence at home but she really didn't want to be dependent on him for protection. Jeff in turn, promised not to hover.

So why this insecurity; she wondered? Shelley had to quash these feelings daily. The Benefit was coming up quickly so she tried to concentrate on writing a fresh act for it as well as helping to organize the event.

This particular night Shelley was restless and couldn't sleep. She was up working at her computer trying to wrap her brain around new material. Bruno was scratching at the sliding doors to go out for a pee. She got up to let the dog out but noticed movement outside her fence.

"Hello is anyone there?" she yelled.

There was no answer, yet the hairs on the back of her neck started to tingle. She could feel the person's eyes bearing down on her.

Once again she yelled out, "Hello!!! Anyone out there; okay you have thirty seconds to show your face or I am dialing 9-1-1."

Shelley heard crunching of foot prints outside the gate. "That's what I thought, ya chicken shit!"

"Who's a chicken shit?" The voice came from behind.

Shelley whirled around to face Jeff. "Crap don't scare me like that moron!"

"I'm the love of your life, and you call me a moron? Should I feel mortally or mildly insulted?

"Mildly will do; I heard something beyond the gate. I was yelling at the lily livered idiot to man up and show himself."

"Want me to check?"

Shelley looked at Jeff pleadingly, "Would you mind?"

"Sure no problem little lady; I live to rescue damsels in distress."

Shelley's groaned. "Oh puleeze, knock off the bad John Wayne/Dudley Do-right impersonations. It doesn't work."

Jeff walked to the back of the yard, opened the rear gate to the alleyway behind and stepped out to look behind Shelley's property. He let out a laugh, and motioned for her to have a look.

Shelley walked to where he was and stifled a giggle. Standing in the alley was a fawn; grazing on a small patch of grass amongst the gravel.

"That's what you nearly called 9-1-1 on." Shelley felt like an idiot but laughed just the same. Both she and Jeff went back to the yard, retrieved Bruno, and went inside.

"Man that was close. I was so sure someone was back there. This whole thing with the serial killer has me jumping out of my skin." Shelley had her arms around Jeff's waist.

"Well I really can't blame you, dear, five people have died and you were attacked less than two weeks ago. Anyone would be a little tense."

"Well, that totally tired me out. I was working on a new bit for the fundraiser. Now I just want to crash and do it tomorrow." Shelley took Jeff's hand and led him to bed. "Let's go try and forget the fact that I nearly called the cops on a deer."

"Why certainly little lady, it'd be a pleasure. As the Duke once said to a leading lady, 'you need to be kissed hard and often'. "

"Oh really, care to tell me what else I need?" Shelley responded seductively.

CHAPTER 35

Hank had been lurking just outside Shelley's backyard. It had been too close for his liking. Nearly getting caught like that was not good.

There had been some bushes on the other side of her fence. The fence had a knot hole he could peek through and see Shelley while she was waiting for her mutt to do his business. She had looked up when he had accidently scuffed his foot against the gravel in the alleyway. He heard her yell out to see if anyone was there and that she was ready to call the cops on him.

The thought had crossed his mind to rush in and take her then. That would have been a daring move; even more daring than the attack on Susanne in Gallagher Park. Even though he'd have to do her without having fun with her first, this idea turned him on somewhat. The thrill of getting caught was more of a rush than actually doing the deed. But breaking into Shelley's back yard to take her and the measly boy-toy would take too much in the way of balls. And there was also the risk that Jeffy-boy would over power him. That would not have been good at all. So he simply waited 'til they had discovered the young fawn grazing in the alleyway before taking off. That had given him a good laugh; the two lovers getting fooled by a mere deer.

Normally Hank would have taken the defenseless animal out for no good reason than too watch it suffer; that was just the bastard in him he supposed. However, the animal had saved his bacon so he decided to be the bigger man and let the animal live. *Mighty white of ya Hank!* He had chuckled to himself. Hank waited patiently for Jeff and Shelley to go back into the house knowing full well they were going in there to get it on. This thought made him want to hurl.

***

Back in the house after some energetic love-making, Jeff and Shelley were lying in bed enjoying each others company.

"Wow that was HOT!" breathed Jeff. "Does feeling like you were being watched turn you on that much?"

"Oh Yeah", Shelley replied; "especially when my voyeur is Bambi!"

"Well if that's the case; we can take this act out to the picnic table and have another go at it."

"Jeff, did anyone tell you what a sex maniac you can be?"

"Says you who just rocked my world five minutes ago; little Miss Nymphet."

"Yeah, well we kinda have to determine some parameters here."

Jeff rolled his eyes at the thought of having one of those talks about relationships; the kind that made the strongest man run fifty miles in the opposite direction. Even though Jeff had been married three times previously the subject still scared the crap out of him.

He steeled himself by starting the topic. "What parameters do we need? We love each other, the sex is phenomenal, and we just fit right."

Shelley agreed with him on all three points; she just wanted to know whether the love and their physical relation ship was more than fleeting. Shelley had invested a lot in past relationships, only to have them go south on her. She loved Jeff; that alone was great and   she wanted more. She could go the distance with this guy; but after two failed marriages and something that happened to the third wife; did he want to try for a fourth?

"I love you Jeff," was what she started with; "I realize you have walked down the aisle three times. Two of those ended in divorce and I don't know what happened to Denise. You don't have to tell me if you don't want to, but I need to know if this is something you want in spite of all that."

Shelley could have gone on, but Jeff shushed her by holding his index finger against her lips.

"You're right. You deserve to know my intentions. You also have the right to know what happened to Mrs. Beals #3. After I tell you; you might not want me. I am bad for you Shell, but I can't help myself. Truth is Denise died."

Shelley was confused. Why would she hate him if his wife had died? Then he told her.

"It was suicide. I came home from a road trip to find her dead in our bed. There was an empty bottle of pills beside her. No real note, just a scribbled sorry on a piece of paper on the desk. I think I pushed her to do it. I was very distrustful after the first two wives left. I was always on the road with my act. I never had any time for her. Denise was miserable.

"That doesn't mean you were to blame," Shelley told him, "it was your job."

"I used my job as a reason to stay away. I figured we couldn't fight if I wasn't there.

I didn't want to stick around and make her life hell. I drank, smoked, and hung out in seedy clubs; instead of subjecting her to all that at home I stayed away. That made her more miserable. I killed her by trying to save her from me."

"Still her dying like that isn't your fault and it doesn't mean that you are bad for me. Unlike Denise I am a comic. I know the business and what is involved; so cut the crap pal you can't scare me!" Shelley reached over and kissed Jeff hard on the lips to further her point.

"Wait Shelley, that's not all. Denise was pregnant. I killed two people."

"No you didn't! Denise killed two people. Shelley wrapped her arms around Jeff to show him all that didn't matter. She felt bad for Denise, sure - but she was an entirely different person, and Jeff was no longer a travelling comic.

"So this means you wanna stick with a beat up old comic has been?"

"On one condition,that you want to stay up late and put up with me rehearsing my acts no matter how cheesy."

"Yes, as long has we can have raging hot monkey sex afterwards."

"Deal!" Shelley rolled over him and showed him the depths of her love.

CHAPTER 36

Things were heating up all over Edmonton. Women were afraid to go out alone at night in the Gallagher Park area. Even though it was a comic that was hit, most people were afraid that some copy cat might get a wise idea and start hitting randomly. As a result of this police patrols had been stepped up in the area surrounding the park.

A couple of guys loading a donations truck at the plaza not far away found a bag of bloody clothes left out side the bin.

"Hey Joe look at this!" Fred said to his partner, while pulling the smelly soiled garment out of the bag.

"What the hell is that?" Joe looked at the outfit splattered with a reddish brown substance. "It could be just paint dude."

"You are a real dumbass Joe! This is blood; it has an iron-like smell to it, it has to be blood. I think the guy who cut up the girl in the park dumped this here and helped himself to a fresh outfit. If that's the case; this here bag of goodies is evidence. I think we should do a public service and turn it in." With this Fred dialed the police on his cell. "If they are grateful they may see clear to pay us a little cash for our discovery."

The party on the other end answered and Fred went into

business mode: "This is Fredriche Driscoll. I drive a donations truck for the diabetes association. My partner Joseph Raines are at the TELUS plaza on Jasper Avenue. Yes officer, I do have a point. We were unloading a donations bin at the west end of the plaza, and we discovered a bag of bloody clothes with the donations. I think it might be connected to the murder in Gallagher Park. I can't be sure but I think it might be worth checking out. We were hoping that it might be something potentially speaking. What do ya mean you don't give rewards for possible evidence? No ma 'am I haven't been doing crack, Yes I am legit! Can you at least send some one to have a look? I didn't have to call this in ya know! Okay great, we'll be here. Thank you ma'am and have a rainbow day." Fred slammed his cell phone shut. "No wonder crime is up in this city;" he said to himself, "the cops are chimps!"

He turned to Joe and told him a car would be over to take evidence and collect the bag, and when he had done that to go to the variety store and grab a couple of sodas for both of them. Joe held out his hand and Fred passed him a fiver. "Cheap ass!" said Joe sourly. The next shift he was asking for Alex. At least he had brains and his own money.

Fred and Joe were sitting in the truck drinking their pops when the CSU car and a couple of patrol officers. Constables Horner and Reid took statements. Fred handed the bag of clothes to the crime scene guy. The team swiped for prints and looked for other evidence around the box. As soon as they had searched the area they thanked Fred and Joe for assistance in the matter. Fred gave them his cell number in case they needed a more detailed statement. The cops nodded their assent that detectives on the case would contact them if needed. Joe didn't say much while the officers questioned them, but after they left he turned to Fred and said he had done the right thing.

The two officers reported to Myra swift about their interview with the two delivery guys. Myra thanked them and they also added that CSU had the bag of bloodied clothes. Hopefully the DNA on them would match Susanne and the case would finally get somewhere. The prints on the knife were being run to see if they matched some one in the system. That would really throw the case wide open. After weeks of so many people dying needlessly, she felt they were finally getting somewhere. The perp in this case had started to make some huge boners. And as a result, evidence would bring him down.

It was time to call the task force together and alert the media that more possible evidence had been found. Myra picked up the phone and set up a meeting for ten a.m. the next morning.

In the meantime she had a date with Vince to do an undercover shift at Comic F/X. She was looking forward to a night away from her desk and just to cut back and do something fun, even though it was still officially police business. People always told her that laughter was the best medicine. Lately, though she was starting to think it was more like poison.

CHAPTER 37

After listening to the evening news, Hank was starting to panic. The item regarding his discarded garments worn during the hit on Susanne had him worried. That and losing his dagger in the bushes at the park ... any more boners like that, the idiot cops would surely nail his ass to the wall.

At least his plan to bomb the fundraiser was still in place. Hank also decided to take them out suicide bomber style. They might be heinous terrorists but the Taliban and the Iraqis weren't stupid by any means. The idea of pulling off major crimes against humanity and evading justice was perfect in his mind. The terrorists were then martyred by their peers. That, in Hank's opinion, would be great. Perhaps other serial killers would hold him in high esteem as well. The greatest victory would be that the whole escapade would blow up in the cops' faces and the last laugh would be his. Cops zilch; Grim reaper one - true justice in his mind.

For all this to happen he also had to step up his plan for Shelley and Jeff. With only a week before the benefit he would have to set his plan in motion quickly. How dare she insinuate in her routine that he was gay? She even had the temerity to call him a wuss. No one should be able to hang out their dirty laundry onstage, thus hurting their loved ones. Yes, it was true she referred to him as Charlie in the act, as that was in fact his first name. What the bitch never realized was the man killing the comics was her ex-lover, the one she had dumped and humiliated two years before. He had trusted her with his heart and what did she do in return? She used their entire relationship as fodder for a good act. Shelley wasn't the only lame-ass comic to do this, everyone did and Hank didn't like it. Now Shelley had a new man, and she was way too happy for his liking. Both of them would feel the knife, but not before Shelley discovered exactly who she was messing with.

Little did Shelley know that he was right under her nose. Changing his name had been a piece of cake. He had taken his middle name, Henry, shortened it to Hank and taken on his mom's maiden name of Cavanaugh. People would probably wonder why he had taken on the name of someone he really couldn't stand; perhaps the irony of all the locked up negative emotions made him do it. That in itself he found to be amusing. Secretly he supposed that if he went down for anything illegal - although he considered what he was doing justified, as pay back for all the pain and suffering he had endured from Shelley using him in her routines - then he would be expected to explain himself and his actions.

If this did happen, he would simply tell them 'Payback is a Bitch'. He would also tell them he was acting on the pain and suffering brought on by other comics – sort of a class action suit. Shrinks would call him nuts, but he didn't care. In any case, if he got his way, the authorities would be too busy trying to pick up the pieces to try and examine what was left of his shattered psyche. This thought made him laugh.

Chapter 33

Once again Comic F/X was packed. Every seat was full and some people were leaning against the bar to see Edmonton's funniest to take the stage.

Shelley was the headliner that night and had her new act ready to try out on the crowd. Jeff had just hired a couple of new comics out of the same pool that spawned Jason and Susanne.

Mike Davis was first up and did a clean pets and family routine which segued into a bit on why some lifestyles just should not go together.

Some lifestyle choices just don't fit together; like gay and nerd. No one told them they have to choose. My friend is a gay nerd. One day while defragging my system he colour coded my desktop items. He met me at the door and said, "I finished early. I discovered your feng was way out of whack with your shuei so I took the liberty of redecorating for you. You might think it odd to climb over your couch to get into the living room, but you will notice an immediate improvement in your karma." Mind you neither my karma nor my midsection was doing well when I ran into the couch in the dark later that night.

It's really hard to build relationships. A gay nerd just doesn't feel comfortable in a gay bar, and if he happens to meet a "kindred spirit" in a Linux club meeting or something, the only option for further development is "Your parents' basement, or mine?"

Other gays question your sexuality because you can't handle the latest dance moves, you still haven't lost the taped up glasses through laser surgery, and you tend to notice the tools and actions of the newest IT service person as he works on the computer instead of the tools and actions revealed by his tight jeans

How do guys figure out that they are in fact gay nerds? Here are some signs you might watch out for if you're not sure.

You like curling because you have guys shouting at you "faster, faster, and faster!" and "Hard. Hard!!"

*You admire an opposing chess player and wonder what his moves would be like after the tournament was over. The nerd in you says I want to **whip** this guy's butt. The gay says I want to whip this guy's **butt.***

You decide the football plays based on how you can get up close and personal to the more interesting players on the opposite team.

A regular guy will join a cheerleading squad to get close to cheerleaders.

A nerd would join because he doesn't want to get hurt playing football. A gay nerd joins to get close to the guys who joined the squad.

The Scrabble club refuses to let you bring refreshments because instead of pretzels and Cheesies you insist on bringing humus, sushi, watercress sandwiches and napkins. You are rejected by other nerds as you have a folded hankie in your breast pocket to match your tie instead of pocket protectors so, to fit in better, you switch to colour coordinated pocket protectors to match your attire.

Your favorite pickup line is in Klingon. "Is that a batlith in your pocket or are you as happy to meet me as I am to meet you?"

Good night every body. This has been great. Enjoy the rest of the night.

The entire audience had loved the act and gave a standing ovation. Dealing with gender orientation was a touchy topic, but he had pulled it off with style.

As Mike got off the stage, he was approached by a guy, and immediately thought he could be heading for a problem. If he wasn't gay himself, he would not have even have attempted a routine like that. The fear was always that he'd get lynched by straight people for being gay or get nabbed and coiffed. Death by perm solution was not an option for him.

"Listen pal" he told the guy. "I am sorry if I offended you with that routine. I don't want to cause any problems."

"Hell no," the other man reacted "I just wanted to tell you, I thought your act was fantastic and wondered if I could buy you a drink."

"Thanks guy but my partner is sitting over there and I don't think he'd appreciate it."

"Not a problem I am here with my partner and we loved your bit. It takes a lot of courage to come out with something like that. You and your fella should come on over and join us." Mike motioned to Russell at the bar to join the two other men, and breathed a sigh of relief that the encounter had gone better than he had envisioned.

Shelley followed up shortly after.

Hey all! Welcome to another fabulous night at Comic F/X. Sit back, and enjoy the three drink minimum. Wally lives for nights like this, big crowd and a chance to emerge from the closet under the stairs. After this we have to round him up and put the ankle band back on so he can't escape.

Shelley looked up and noticed Wally giving her the finger. That was his signal that he enjoyed the verbal abuse, cleverly disguised as comic shtick!

All that having been said, anyone here ever do home renovations with your spouse? Fun isn't it?

There ought to be a section in a prenuptial agreement that stipulates that no decorating, painting, renovating or just plain rearranging furniture should be done with your beloved. If you don't have a pre-nup, you're screwed. In fact, I am willing to go one better and say that it should have been the eleventh commandment.

With this there were cheers from the men and collective groans from the women. Myra and Vince were in back, cheering for Shelley.

Shelley waited for the uproar to cool down and continued:

Come on girls, admit it you really don't want to go on for months hearing your guy rant about how the man cave is 'sacred and hallowed ground' that shouldn't be desecrated by female sensibilities like plants and other frou-frou. He complains that your strategically placed air fresheners interfere with the ambient stench of stale beer and cigar smoke.

We really don't want the incessant whining that occurs while we waffle over what colour schemes go best with our selections of summer tank tops. After all we want to blend in with our décor. Please guys deal with it! It's a girl thing!

This time the women roared with laughter and the guys booed.

Imagine this, you come home one day after a long eight hour shift, and your guy has taken the liberty of painting the whole house the same colour. Obviously the paint chip taped to the wall of each room didn't matter at all…Didn't do much for my karma and had a lot to do with the fact that he didn't get any that night.

There was more laughing from the women.

So I sent him outside to commune with his power tools with much male posturing, and whining about being the injured party. The dog had her front paws over her ears, since she was also unsympathetic to his cause.

He also complains that in addition to painting and renovating you also needed to buy a new living room ensemble and dining suite to replace the perfectly good junk you have had for years. Says it's enough furniture to house a discount furniture outlet. You also have the treat of listening to him gripe over the fact that the garage sale you are holding to sell his crap falls on the opening day of trout fishing season, and that you expect him to preside over it as further torture.

At this point, the men were enraged and it looked like a riot was going to break out in the club —*So ladies, that alone is proof, that married people are not destined to survive home renovations.*

Shelley got off the stage and ducked out the back door before the men got the chance to lynch her.   She snuck back in the front. She thought that maybe that was a little over the top, but it was fun to do from the female perspective, for a change.

CHAPTER 39

Shelley's routine wasn't as good as it had felt before she got up and did it. She'd have to tweak it some before the big night at the Benefit. She went over it in her mind on the way home from the club. She remembered a time when she and Charlie were going to redecorate the house. That had happened about two months before he left. He, like the guy in her routine, had postured and complained about all the work it would cause and what it would cost. In the end, nothing had been done and they had stopped speaking. After that Charlie had started to whine about everything she did and even resented her career as a comedian. He stated that she was just using him as 'good material' for her act; yes *Charlie bad sex does make for great comedy. Thanks for the memories dude.*

He used to go watch her at the clubs in Calgary and Vancouver before they finally sold the house and parted company. He left her the house when he walked out. He said that all comics sounded alike and made their names on the backs of their so called loved ones' feelings and it was all bullshit. He even gave her an ultimatum –the comedy act or their relationship. Being that the act was more fun than he was, she chose the former.

Shelley had known that Charlie was a little off going into the relationship, but ignored his quirks in deference to her feelings for him. Looking back she now realized there was something very odd about that man.

Shelley was still in a reverie about Charlie when she realized the guy outside the club the night Jason was killed walked an awful lot like Charlie used to. She knew there had been something familiar about that man. Shelley parked the car in her driveway and raced into her house. She dumped her purse on the kitchen counter and went searching for her memory box. It was in the closet in the office. Shelley went digging through the pictures and found what she was looking for. There was a picture of Charlie, unsmiling and with an attitude 'There you took the picture now F-off!' Damn who do you look like? She looked at the bulletin board over her desk. There hung the mug shot of the man matching Jay's description. Holy crap! Charlie could be the serial killer!! Could his outright disdain for comedians have pushed him to this? Had her using him as the brunt of her jokes made him into a knife wielding monster?

Right underneath the picture was his high school graduation diploma, given to her years ago. The name Charles Henry Danforth stood out. She also went and grabbed a past income tax return that she remembered he'd left behind. Why he'd left it, she couldn't recall, but it would certainly come in handy now. It had Charlie's Social Insurance Number on it. That could be traced to find a current address for him if needed. Shelley knew what she had to do for the sake of the dead comics and possible future victims. She was going to the cops with the information. But she was praying she wasn't right.

Chapter 40

Shelley was risking a speeding ticket as she raced to the precinct. Then she remembered that she had spotted Vince Vetters and Myra Swift at the club that night. Division 74 was right down town near Comic F/X and was easy to find. She called Jeff on the cell to meet her at the station as soon as he was done at the club. He wanted details as to why she was rushing off to the police at that late hour. Shelley promised to fill him in when he got there, before hanging up.

Shelley was wracking her brain to remember details about Charlie that might just help the police find and stop him if he was the killer. She was sickened by the very thought that the man she had spent four years with might be responsible for the recent carnage.

She would turn in the information she had, but continue to look for more. There was a box of Charlie's stuff still in her closet that he had never come back for. Maybe there were things in there they could use as well.

Shelley parked in the lot and ran into the station house. She nearly ran into Borneo on his way out.

"Whoa Miss Morgan! Where's the fire?"

"Sorry Officer Borneo, but I have some information as to the identity of the killer."

"Really? That's fantastic! Come on - Myra Swift is in, doing her report for her shift at your club. I'm sure she'll want to see this. She said that you guys really knocked 'em dead tonight."

"Good. I thought the men were going to have my ass in a sling for my home renovations act."

Borneo led her through the squad room and into Swift's office. He knocked at her door.

"Detective Swift?" Mike tried to get her attention as Myra was typing on the computer.

Myra looked up. "Yes officer, if you're still trying to peddle stale donuts and that sad excuse for coffee, you can forget it."

"Now would I do something so heinous to my favorite superior officer, when I refuse to drink the stuff myself?"

"Who knows? Now what can I do for you? It's been a long day, and I want to get home."

"Miss Morgan has some information she thinks could be useful in the Comic Killer case."

This definitely caught Myra's attention. She quickly called the captain's office and asked him to join them in the conference room. He was there with in minutes. Shelley started to tell her story just as Jeff was ushered in. Myra and the captain listened intently as Shelley recounted her years with Charlie. She showed them his picture and set it beside the composite mug of the killer. The captain and the detective were amazed by the similarities between Shelley's former lover and the suspect.

The captain asked Shelley to bring in any other pertinent information about Mr. Danforth. He also asked Shelley and Jeff to attend the next meeting of the task force scheduled for the next day.

Shelley and Jeff left the info with the police and headed home to locate and bring in the box of Charlie's stuff.

But despite all of this, Shelley clung to the hope that they were wrong.

CHAPTER 41

Although she was both physically and emotionally exhausted, Shelley went home from the police station that night and dug out the box of Charlie's things from the storage room down stairs. She should have thrown this stuff out after he left, but thought better of it. Now she was glad she had kept it, because it might contain proof that he was the killer.

Shelley also made a list of all the things she knew about Charlie.

His mother had died when he was in his early twenties, before Shelley had hooked up with him. He never really wanted to talk about her and stated that they hadn't been close. Anyone with a degree in psychology would argue that this was typically Freudian thinking. He never expounded on the reasons why he disliked his mother so much and Shelley really didn't want to push.

The box contained a long copy of his birth certificate stating that one Florence Alma Cavanaugh was listed as mother and the father was Charles Henry Danforth. That could be useful so Shelley put it in the keeper pile.

There were no records of his mother's death, but his father's death certificate was present. Another possibly useful bit so she added that to the pile. There were pictures of him and his dad where Charlie looked happy and carefree; however, in the photos of him with his mother his countenance was grim, indicating he'd rather be somewhere else. She might include a few of those, just in case a police psychologist might find them interesting.

Halfway through her search Jeff came into the den to see how she was faring and asked when she was coming to bed.

"Hm?" Shelley was totally engrossed and not really focusing on Jeff.

"Are you going to pull an all-nighter with this stuff?" Jeff was not exactly sure if her searching was doing any good at all. For all he knew, Shelley was just dredging up a lot of bad memories of a failed relationship. It might be a waste of time, but he had to let her do it. Maybe he was wrong and something linking Charlie to the killings might be there.

"I'm almost done, Jeff. I am hoping beyond hope that I am very wrong about this and I was not sleeping with a monster of my own creation."

"What do you mean? Do you think you caused him to slip over the edge and do all these things?"

"It's a possibility I can't afford to ignore. There were signs near the end where he really hated my dream to be a comedian and refused to listen to me rehearse my act. This was especially true after I used him as the butt of a few jokes. Maybe I hit a nerve and just didn't know when to stop. He hated my act and refused to go and watch me or anyone else perform."

"Do yourself a favor;" Jeff advised her, "don't speculate on this too much. Let the professionals deal with this. I want you fresh and in good shape for the benefit. I am saying this as your lover and your boss.

"Besides I have a really good way to make you forget all this." Jeff said conspiratorially.

Shelley looked at the longing in Jeff's eyes and knew there was just no way of skirting the issue and perhaps a romp would be good medicine. She made a deal with him to present the data at the meeting and the leave psychoanalyzing to the pros. Jeff told her she was doing the right thing, took her hand, and led her to the bedroom for his own version of therapy.

Chapter 42

The task force meeting began, and Shelley took the podium and outlined her theories that her ex, Charlie, and the serial killer might be one and the same. After she was finished her presentation, she fielded questions from the floor. All her points had good bones and the task force was willing to send feelers out for Charles Danforth or any of the following aliases: Hank or Henry Danforth, Chuck Cavanaugh or Hank Cavanaugh. Someone would be responsible for sending all the above names through the Canadian National Criminal Justice research service and even the FBI registry in the States. Hopefully something matching his description would come up.

The picture Shelley had brought in indeed looked enough like the police artist's sketch that it would be broadcast on the news. Be on lookout for (BOLOS) were also issued to the entire police force. Also the prints found on the knife and the DNA found on the bloody clothes would be run through the system as well. The blood would most likely be the victims' but there had been skin found under Susanne's finger nails during the autopsy; maybe there was enough DNA for a match.

Shelley still hoped she was wrong about this, but she feared if she didn't help she would be dead wrong.

Jeff said Shelley was taking a big risk and requested some sort of protection against possible retaliation. If the killer was indeed her former lover he might not appreciate the fact that she had turned on him. Shelley could be in serious danger.

The chief arranged for around the clock surveillance for Shelley at both her house and at the club. Jeff decided he would also shadow her 24/7 to keep her safe. Shelley really didn't want that much attention but that's the price she paid for opening this can of worms. There was no use debating or even grumbling about it. Jeff and the police were determined to protect her as a source. As there was only circumstantial evidence at best, the police could not announce Charlie as a suspect, merely a person of interest at this point.

After the meeting was over Shelley asked Myra and Lissa to have coffee. She wanted to pick their brains on the possibility that her great desire to be a comic had caused her to ignore signs that it had pushed Charlie over the edge, thus sending him on the killing spree.

"Did my zeal for fame create this knife wielding monster? Should I have listened to him and not bashed him in my routines?"

Myra placed her hand over Shelley's. "Honey, you had no idea that Charlie harbored issues about this. There is no possible way that it was a conscious effort to emasculate him in your routine. If you had known this really bothered him, I doubt you would have been that cruel."

"I can't be entirely sure of that, Myra. Near the end of our relationship, everything I did was pushing him away. I basically told him *'Screw you!'* at every turn. Whatever he did in the last months we were together was getting on my nerves. The more he whined the more things I did just to piss him off. Finally he just left and frankly I was relieved. He was so stoic about the whole thing. Maybe it was just the calm before the storm."

Lissa made it clear that she agreed with the detective's opinion that Shelley could never have known it would result in Charlie losing it and going on a stabbing spree.

Detective Swift was happy to set Shelley up to talk with the staff psychologist since he was more equipped to reassure her that she was not in any way responsible for Charlie's breakdown. Shelley said she'd think about it further. She really just wanted to concentrate in the upcoming benefit for now and let the police do their job in catching the criminal responsible.

CHAPTER 43

The agreement Shelley and Jeff had was for him to accompany her on all outings no matter how trivial. This way her safety was ensured even if Charlie/Hank was dumb enough to attempt an attack with Jeff present. Jeff could counter attack or at least call 9-1-1 for back-up.

Unfortunately Shelley had needed to venture out for some emergency supplies and couldn't wait for Jeff. Jeff was a great guy but she didn't quite trust him to pick up feminine supplies and get it right; not yet anyway. Maybe she should include this bit in an act somewhere. Shelley was busy putting her things in the back of her SUV when she felt an arm around her neck. She could tell it was Charlie by both his natural scent and the scent of his cologne. That's one thing that hadn't changed in the years gone by. Ironically the woody scent was the only thing she ended up missing about him.

Shelley had felt confident that the parking lot was crowded enough to avert a confrontation with a possible assailant that she didn't think twice about going to the store. However, she currently found herself in a precarious position. She'd obviously overestimated his intelligence or Charlie had grown some cajones since their last encounter. "Don't move or I'll cut you where you stand," Charlie/Hank was hissing in her ear.

"Really, Charlie; Is that the nicest thing you can come up with after such a long time?"

"Shut up Shelley, and stop trying to be so tough. By the time I am done with you, you'll be a quivering mass of fear. No, slash that, by the time I am done with you and your boyfriend, you'll both be dead!! First of all, before I do that, I plan to impress upon you that all this murdering comics shit is your fault."

Shelley tried to laugh at the skewed logic of her assailant but one false move would mean choking.

Charlie started again. "On a count of three, I want you to turn around and face me. I want to explain why I did all this to those comics, and you will see that their blood is on your hands. Try anything funny, and I kill you now."

Shelley did as instructed and turned to face him. He had changed some over the past three or four years.

"Charlie, do we really need to do this here in the parking lot? " Shelley was looking for a way to alert someone to get help before Charlie could notice what she was up to and act upon it. Obviously he was showing more balls than brains here by trying to discuss personal matters in the Supersaver lot.

"Why the hell not? You never hesitated to air my dirty laundry on stage, did you? It was never any problem for you to emasculate me in a club full of people. I told you countless times how embarrassing it was to have our relationship used as fodder for a stand up act."

"Ha! Well if you were so damned pissed off at me, why kill the others?"

"Because all you damn comedians do the same thing; nothing is sacred. Every one does it and it is so wrong!"

"Yes Charlie, I agree, every one does it at one time or another. But other comic's spouses or partners don't go on a killing spree because of it. I refuse to own those deaths. That's your doing. You have robbed so many unfortunate people of a future with loved ones because of your issues. Some of those people you killed were talented people with a good future. Some of those people had families and won't ever see their sons or daughters again. Most of all, they were my friends and I hate you for that alone!"

Shelley was hoping she could distract him while he was on a tirade. She could call 9-1-1 keep the attendant on the line or call Jeff and do the same hoping he'd find them and call 9-1-1 for her. She was not going to let this asshole take her here or anywhere else for that matter. He had serious problems that needed fixing.

In the distance she heard sirens approaching. Charlie/Hank was alerted to the sound.

"You Bitch! You called the cops!" Charlie lunged at her but Shelley kicked out and hit him in the sternum and he went down. He tried to grab at her leg but she backed out of the way too fast. He was trying to regain his balance and attempting to get off his knees. Shelley was alert to this and sent out a flying side kick to his shoulder. This sent Charlie onto his back gasping for air. Shelley yelled for help to subdue her attacker at this point and proceeded to call the authorities. "That wasn't me Charlie, but you can rest assured that help will be forthcoming shortly."

Lying on the ground, Charlie was screaming obscenities at her as well as the guys trying to subdue him. Shelley knelt down beside him and told him to shut up. "I have heard enough whining for one day. Life sucks Charlie; Deal with it!"

Now that the police were on the way she called Jeff's cell.

He answered on the first ring; "Shelley where the hell are you? When I got home you weren't there, and the cops on surveillance had no clue."

"I'm at the Supersaver. I had to get something and grabbed dinner fixings too. I thought I'd be safe. I'm okay, the situation is under control; just come over here, I need help with some excess baggage."

Chapter 44

Jeff and the cops arrived at the same time. There were five squad cars and an unmarked containing Myra Swift and the captain. Shelley had alerted the 9-1-1 operator that it was the comic killer and he could be armed and dangerous. Cassway and Borneo were in one of the squad cars and Davis and Dumais in one of the others. Davis was calling for a couple of ambulances; one for Shelley and the other for Charlie/Hank.

Jeff rushed up and grabbed Shelley into a hug. He could have lost her in this battle. He was pissed at her stupidity in going out without him. At the same time he was glad to see she was alright. He wanted to rip a strip off her for taking off, but there were more important things at stake.

The police had Charlie draped over the hood of one of the squad cars as one of the officers frisked him and cuffed him. They had found a dagger much like the one used in many of the stabbings. A warrant was out allowing them to search his house for more weapons, and further evidence. A crime unit was scouring the premises and would call if they found anything significant to the case. He had a head wound that needed patching up and would be transported by ambulance with one of the officers accompanying him.

Shelley walked over to the other ambulance to be checked over for any serious wounds. They decided she was fine, and she went on her own back to her car to take the groceries home. She promised to be at the station to give a statement later that evening.

The captain and Myra had said it could wait until morning, but Shelley stated that she just wanted to get it done and then go home and crash.

Jeff followed her home and helped her get the bags out of the car.

Neither one of them spoke until Shelley looked at Jeff.

"Okay, let me have it!! It was a damn stupid move to go out on my own. I'm sorry."

"Yeah it was. I should be mad at you for pulling a boneheaded move. Frankly I am just relieved that I don't have to kill the son of a bitch for hurting you. I am so happy that it was him on the ground and not you. How did you manage to deal with him like that?"

Shelley was standing proud. "Let me tell ya, those self defense lessons I took really paid off. Twice in three weeks my WENDO really came in handy. I just waited for the opportunity to take him down while he was ranting and raving. What really helped was the siren. That distracted him and BAM he went down like a stone."

"Remind me never to piss you off, woman!" Jeff laughed.

"I had more fun things in mind other than enraging me, but alas I want to go give my statement to the cops while it's still fresh."

"Sounds like a good plan, then my dear lady I am going take you out; wine and dine you then romance the socks off you."

"Just my socks?" Shelley asked Jeff, hopefully.

"Well, that and anything else that wants to fall off."

"Well, Mister, I think it's a fantastic idea. But let's get the nasty stuff done first; then I promise I'm all yours."

"For the next twenty five years or so?" Jeff was looking at her intently as he said this.

"Is this a marriage proposal?" Shelley was incredulous that Jeff would want to dive into a fourth marriage.

"It could be, we don't have to decide now. We can wait 'til after we deal with the fundraiser and with the Charlie problem. Let's get the bastard behind bars, and then think about it."

"Deal!" They kissed on it to seal the deal –there would be more time to get romantic later. and headed out the door.

CHAPTER 45

After having gotten Charlie/Hank checked out at the hospital, the police escorted him back to the division and threw him into an interrogation room to stew for a bit.

The Captain and Myra were going to try the tactic of telling Charlie that Shelley recorded the tirade in the parking lot so it might be best to confess. Not only that, they had him dead to rights on the bombs found in his house and the collection of knives possibly used in the murders. They were prepared to roast the squirrel over an open fire and watch him squirm.

Shelley was currently giving her statement to another homicide detective and it would be added to the pile of evidence that would ensure Charlie/Hank would not see daylight until retirement age. However, if a defense requested treatment in a psychiatric ward for the next twenty-odd years, that would be fine as well. As long as the public didn't have to deal with him for quite some time, it would be a good conviction.

The Captain went in first, as Myra watched and listened just outside the room.

"Mr. Danforth or is it Mr. Cavanaugh these days?" The Captain had all the particulars on the case before him. An assistant crown attorney was present to make sure the police were doing things by the book. The duty counsel had been called to represent the accused as he didn't have access to his own lawyer. The only lawyer Charlie had ever dealt with was a real estate lawyer so he had no criminal attorney at his disposal.

"My name is Hank Cavanaugh; I ceased being Charles Danforth since the bitch betrayed me."

"Which bitch are you referring to Mr. Cavanaugh?" The Captain was quickly losing patience with Hank as he had copped a whiney 'poor me' attitude all the way over from the mall. If it weren't considered police brutality, he would have let Myra bitch slap him.

"Miz Morgan. If you ask me, it's her you should be questioning, not me." Hank spat on the floor as he uttered her name.

"Why is that?" This idiot was really pissing him off. "Shelley didn't kill five people, you did!"

"If it hadn't been for her callous disregard for my feelings, and if she had heeded my request to quit using our relationship in her routine, I wouldn't have had to take my anger out on those comedians. It's really her fault I am here at all. And it wasn't just Shelley. All comics use the humiliation and suffering of so called loved ones to advance their careers. She and others like her made us all look like wimps."

The Captain really wanted to laugh at him. It had been a long time since he had heard a 'the devil made me do it' rationalization or a 'they had it coming to them' excuse. He could write a friggin' book on the pleas he heard about why perps went postal or cold bloodedly murdered a spouse or an innocent bystander.

"Hank," he said as he got in the killers face, "We both know why you're here. You maliciously took the lives of five innocent people. I don't give a rats ass whether you have poor impulse control or just weren't feeling 'regular' at the time. It was you plunging the knife into those people, not Ms Morgan as you accuse. So just cut the shit and do the right thing; admit you are entirely culpable for each death.

"We also have you for weapons, as we found a box of daggers in your basement. Not only that, the crime scene unit found a box of pipe bombs, ready for God knows what. You can explain those later. To top that off your ex-girlfriend is swearing in a complaint of assault and uttering threats. Face it creep, you're so screwed."

"Or what?" Hank spat at him, his face blazing.

"Or I can easily call in Detective Vetters. Yeah you remember the name. He's the brother of one of the victims. My friend and colleague Vince would love to come in here and rip your head from your shoulders and tear you a new butt hole while he's at it. Trust me he's mad enough to do it. I am pissed enough to let him, but I won't! Do ya want to know why? I'd lose my badge, my pension and you aren't worth it!"

Hank was quaking in his chair so badly, his cuffed hand was rattling violently against the metal table. He was ready to soil himself. Gone was the false bravado and posturing he had pulled off in the squad car on the way over here. He was physically slumped in his chair.

"Just don't put me in general population, please, I am begging you." Hank was crying fearfully now.

"I am sorely tempted trust me! I'd love to see those guys down there, with equally bad impulse control, have their way with your sorry ass." The captain was visibly fuming. "However, we are putting you in solitary, as I and the families of the folks you murdered want to see you pay for this, every day for the rest of your miserable life."

The Captain turned and stomped out of the room. Outside the interrogation room he told the guard to take Hank to a cell, no roommates.

"Why do him any favors?" Myra stated scornfully.

"Those animals will zero in and rip him to shreds down there. They might be common criminals but they still like their comedy; he doesn't stand a chance. Come on, let's go tell Vince that we caught Phil's killer and grab a beer. Lord knows I need one!"

CHAPTER 46

The news spread quickly that the comic killer was in custody. All the evidence found in Charlie/Hanks house was quite useful. The daggers matched the wounds in the victims, as well, and his butcher knife matched the one used on Dave Feener and Phil Vetters. The bombs found in his closet were collected and destroyed. The diaries where he had written his dark ugly thoughts were enough to burn him. There was a collective sigh of relief in the stand-up community.

The task force summed up their case and handed matters over to the prosecution and defense for purposes of discovery. The defense was trying for a plea of insanity and Charlie still wanted to launch a civil suit against Shelley for pain, suffering and defamation of character. Jeff's lawyer assured her she had no worries.

"He doesn't have a leg to stand on. He'd have to have an ounce of character worth defaming to make that stick"

Shelley chuckled. Though she felt a modicum of sympathy for her ex-boyfriend's issues, she did not feel that she caused his problems. After consulting with the police psychologists and having a long talk with her brother Bob, Shelley truly believed that Charlie's problems were present long before she came along. He just treated her as a scapegoat because he didn't want to own his issues. The only person he could possibly blame for his trauma was his long-dead mother Florrie. The defense was shooting for an insanity plea and a competency hearing to determine his fitness to stand trial. Shelley wanted to see him get any help he could, but she wanted justice served for the dead at the same time.

***

Plans were in place for the fundraiser in honor of the dead comedians. The event was getting big air time and tickets were sold out across the city. People were coming from Calgary and a few other places. The way things were going the convention centre might not be large enough. There was talk of moving the venue to Rexall Place while the Oilers were travelling.

The comic community was keeping the moratorium on slasher jokes, out of respect for the bereaved families and the case as a whole. Several comics grumbled as they would have liked to have taken potshots at the killer. However, wanting to keep their jobs at the various comedy clubs in Edmonton and Calgary, they agreed not to.

Finally Friday came along, and the Benefit was the main event. Shelley and her fellow comedians from Comic F/X and Laff Attak were gearing up and prepping new material. Jeff and Ron Cambridge, the owners of the two local clubs, agreed to co-host the event. Phil Vetters' brother Vince was going to give a speech on behalf of all the families thanking the community as a whole for supporting them during the dark days. He also thanked his colleagues on the police force for their swift action in solving the case.

One by one the comics took the stage to pay homage to their fallen comrades. A montage of pictures of Dave, Phil, Jason, Squid and Susanne flashed on a screen behind the stage.

Shelley was the last to take the stage with hopefully, a show stopping, breakout routine of material.

Good evening, Edmonton! To our friends from the south in Calgary, 'enjoy the Chinooks while they last guys, you'll be back in your long johns by Monday.'

Boos arose from the audience at that comment.

Haven't seen this much excitement in Edmonton since the Great One played for our Oilers. Our red mile hasn't been this crowded since the Stanley Cup last came through the City…since when? Last June—what do I know –I am a woman! I really haven't cared too much about who scored on who and when. I have enough trouble keeping on top of that on General Hospital. Soaps, I mean really, men make fun of us girls for watching those damn things, but make them miss an NHL game and all Hell breaks lose. Thankfully my current main squeeze is not a big sports fan. I have been really busy making him forget what a two point spread really looks like.

Wolf whistles emitted from the men in the crowd and the women laughed.

Have you ever noticed how despondent a guy gets when his favorite team loses? Everything in our house used to stand still on Saturday nights. My brothers, the horny little chimps that they were, didn't even want to see anything sexy. The only people they cared about getting any action at all were Gretzky and Messier making sure that Grant Fuhr wasn't getting any. The only thing my brothers got even close to getting orgasmic about was stick handling and a five minute penalty against the opponent. I used to think my brothers suffered from ADD as kids, I have since rethought this. Maybe it was a bad case of NHL. My girlfriends and I thought that if it was all that important to our guys, they could handle their own sticks.

Yeah that was a bit crude I know, but sometimes girls you really have to speak the only four languages a guy really understands, sports, sex, cars and beer. If you get good enough at it to get all four in one sentence, you might just get somewhere. Don't even try to have a conversation with a guy about ' your relationship' or 'taking things to the next level' unless you are prepared to sink to the level of the dreaded sports metaphors and threaten a total smack down if one night a week is not dedicated to a dinner and a movie of your choice.

This is the advice I am going to give my future daughter should I be fortunate enough to have one. Sure I'll have the usual talk about love and respect, STDs and birth control. That's important stuff, but the real lesson is engaging in the rules of marriage. I have retooled the old saying about the hand that rocks the cradle is the hand that rules the world. (The women in the audience cheered here.)

Yeah, it really should read as the hand that holds the remote is the hand that rules the world. As soon as we wrestle the damn thing from the hands of our guys we have them by the cajones!

Night all you've been great!

The audience stood up and applauded the cast of comedians as they took the stage for a final bow.

Shelley came off the stage straight into Jeff's arms.

"You, my love, were a star out there!"

"Ya think so? I was kind of unsure of handling a sports themed act as I am not a sports fan."

"Well ya did your homework well and it worked. The guys loved the hockey stuff and the women ate up the liberated material—A Win/Win situation. At the risk of sounding crude, you're the only one I need doing any stick handling."

"I'll take that into consideration, say for the next 40 or 50 years?" Shelley smiled and waited for his reaction.

"You mean?" He was really starting to think she was not ready for further commitment especially after the recent events. But here she was saying yes to his proposal.

Shelley was nodding and tears were running down her face. "Yes if you want to spend the rest of your days with a cranky, hormonal, caffeine addicted comedienne."

Jeff lifted Shelley off the ground in an immense bear hug. "I don't even mind being the butt of a few good natured bits."

"Well it's going to happen anyway whether I am on stage or not so get used to it."

Shelley kissed him and he smiled. Jeff and Shelley left the stadium to go and party with the rest of the comedians at Laff Attak. The members of the task force had been invited to the after party.

Screw fame as a comedian; Jeff knew at that moment he had made it with this woman.

That, he decided, was all he really needed

Epilogue 2008

"Holy shit!" Corey, the bartender at Comic F/X was shocked. He had remembered that something bad had happened years ago. Jeff's explanation pretty much brought it all back.

"So you're saying that because Shelley's ex-boyfriend couldn't take a joke, he went on a killing spree. What a nut-job!"

"Yep basically that's the long and short of it." Jeff was nursing a gin and tonic and was now watching his very pregnant wife spouting jokes about pregnancy and disappearing waistlines.

She still had the chops she had five years earlier, and she was still the sexiest comic in town even with the baby bump.

Corey still had loads of questions. "So what happened to the fruitcake? Is he still doing time?"

Charlie's lawyer had tried to get him into a psychiatric treatment centre, but a jury of his peers deemed that he was totally cognizant of his actions. In the sentencing part of his trial, it was decided he was sentenced to twenty five years to be served concurrently. Basically it added up to five years per victim. Time served in the general population. He lost his civil case against Shelley for pain and suffering. He was essentially laughed out of court.

"No, he died in prison. Some of the hardest criminals still have a sense of humor. They lynched him in the yard, and nailed him for killing the comedians. They didn't kill him but he took his own life later that day. Seems the powers that be decided he really didn't need solitary, as much as he thought he did. Apparently the incident in the yard was too hard on his delicate psyche. The guys who attacked him had years tacked onto each of their sentences for the assault. That didn't change their day to day prison life. They even held a Last Comic Standing type of competition. And Shelley got over the trauma enough to go visit the prison and gave the guys tips on comedy. She thought the guys got a lot out of the experience. She is now able to talk about the three months of hell in her routines."

Corey chuckled, "So what happened to Wally, the previous bartender?"

Jeff was laughing too at this point. "That's the best part! Remember how Wally was the brunt of a lot of jokes here? He got sick of that, quit and went on the road as a comedian. He decided he was just as funny as the rest of us, did a few open mike nights, and was discovered by an agent who happened to be visiting that night. Lucky frigging break, if ya ask me."

"No shit!" said Corey "Maybe I should try that."

Jeff looked at him gravely and shook his head. "No son, stick to bartending. You're not that funny!"

Corey frowned at him for a second, and then nodded, "You're right, life might be hard, but comedy can kill you."

Glossary

Perps—perpetrators of any crime

'unsub.' stands for 'unknown subject' which is FBI speak for unknown perpetrator

M.O.—Modus operandi—motive for committing a crime.

Chapter 4—

"Out here in the field, I fight for my meals. I put my back into my livin'

I don't need to fight, to prove I'm right. I don't need to be forgiven."

lyrics being sung by Mike in the squad car is from Baba O'Reilly—a song by The Who

About the Author

Karen Vaughan lives in Peterborough Ontario with her husband Jim and one cat. Dead comic standing is her second novel. Her first novel Dead on arrival garnered praise from friends, family and online gamers. She also enjoys doing crafts and other hobbies.